Twelve hou...
fragrance of ...

Of hearing her ...
June—who'd been sitting across the aisle.
Twelve desperately long hours when he'd had
to suffer the torment of feeling his body
responding in a way it hadn't done in years
had been too much for anyone to contend
with. He'd hoped things might have improved
when she'd fallen asleep, and they had for a
while, until her head had slipped sideways
and ended up on his shoulder.

That had been the final straw, the one that had
broken this particular camel's back. Shiloh
hadn't felt even a smattering of guilt about
waking her when he'd got up to go to the
bathroom because he'd had no choice. It had
been either that or…

He wasn't even going down that route!

Jennifer Taylor lives in the north-west of England with her husband Bill. She had been writing Mills & Boon® romances for some years, but when she discovered Medical Romances™ she was so captivated by these heart-warming stories that she set out to write them herself! When she's not writing or doing research for her latest book, Jennifer's hobbies include reading, travel, walking her dog and retail therapy (shopping!). Jennifer claims all that bending and stretching to reach the shelves is the best exercise possible.

Recent titles by the same author:

SURGEON IN CRISIS

BY
JENNIFER TAYLOR

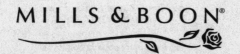

MILLS & BOON®

All the characters in this book have no existence outside the imagination of the author, and have no relation whatsoever to anyone bearing the same name or names. They are not even distantly inspired by any individual known or unknown to the author, and all the incidents are pure invention.

First published in Great Britain 2004
Harlequin Mills & Boon Limited,
Eton House, 18-24 Paradise Road, Richmond, Surrey TW9 1SR

© Jennifer Taylor 2004

ISBN 0 263 83892 7

Set in Times Roman 10½ on 13 pt.
03-0404-42527

Printed and bound in Spain
by Litografia Rosés, S.A., Barcelona

CHAPTER ONE

'YOU must be Rachel. We were told to expect you. Quick, Ted, reel her in before she escapes!'

Rachel Hart gasped as two sets of hands reached out of the doorway and hauled her into the warehouse. 'What on earth d'you think you're doing?' she demanded as soon she was released.

'Making sure you don't have time for any second thoughts.' The young man who had opened the door to her grinned. 'You'd be *amazed* how many people reach this point then suddenly change their minds.'

'No wonder if that's how you normally greet them,' Rachel retorted tartly.

She took a deep breath but she'd felt nervous even before this had happened and it was hard to appear calm. Several times on her way to the docks, in fact, she'd found herself wondering if she'd been mad to volunteer for this job. After all, she'd been a sister on the children's ward at Dalverston General Hospital for the last eight years so what did she know about working in the aftermath of a disaster? She'd only ever seen a hurricane on television, and as for an earthquake…

'Here we go, Bill. Lock the door before she does a runner.'

Rachel blinked when the other young man spoke. She frowned as she turned to him. 'Why do you think that I'm going to leave?'

'Because you're starting to wonder what you've let yourself in for and that's *always* a bad sign,' he replied so dryly that Rachel laughed.

'How did you know what I was thinking?'

'Because it's my job to know what people think.' He held out his hand. 'Brian Parker, resident shrink. I'm the guy who goes in after you lot have finished patching folk up and help them try to make sense of what's happened.'

'Nice to meet you, Brian,' Rachel replied, shaking his hand. She looked at him quizzically. 'I'm sorry to be so dim but if your name's Brian then why did your friend call you Ted just now?'

'Ah, that's just a little game we like to play. We all have nicknames to do with characters from films, you see.' He grinned at her. 'I'm Ted and Daniel over there is known to all and sundry as Bill. We chose the names because we keep having all these excellent adventures...'

'Oh, I see! My niece absolutely adores that film!' Rachel exclaimed. 'So which other characters do you have working here?'

'Oh, there's dozens of them. They come and go according to who's on the team at any given time,' Brian explained cheerfully. 'We all have full-time jobs and just take leave of absence as and when we're needed. It means there's a constant change-over of staff.'

'All apart from our revered leader, of course,' Daniel put in. 'Shiloh's in charge of each and every mission so he's always around.'

'Do you mean Dr Smith?' Rachel glanced at the letter she was holding. 'I was told to report to him when I arrived but before I do, tell me how he got the name Shiloh.'

'Because my parents had way too much imagina-tion, I'm afraid.'

Rachel swung round when she heard a gravelly voice behind her and gasped when she saw the man who was walking towards them. It was rather dark in the warehouse but from what little she could see he was simply huge!

Her gaze flew from the top of his blond head to the tips of his booted feet and she gulped. So this was Dr John Smith, acclaimed surgeon and head of Worlds Together, an agency that specialised in help-ing the victims of natural disasters throughout the world. She'd heard a lot about him—several of the broadsheets had published features about his work in the past few years so she'd even seen photographs as well. However, nothing she'd seen had prepared her for the sheer physical impact he made on her as he came to join them. For the first time in ages Rachel couldn't think of a thing to say so it was left to him to take charge, which he did with an ease that showed he was used to the effect he had on people.

'John is an old family name. There are John Smiths stretching back for centuries, apparently. My parents were keen to carry on the tradition when I was born but decided to add something a little more memorable and came up with Shiloh, for their sins.' He shrugged, his massive shoulders lifting beneath the thick, cable-knit sweater he was wearing. 'I spent most of my formative years in fear of anyone finding out, but my secret was unearthed eventually and I've been stuck with the name ever since. If you prefer to call me John, though, it's fine by me.'

He smiled and Rachel felt the floor suddenly lift beneath her feet when she saw the warmth in his eyes. It was such an odd sensation that once again she couldn't think of anything to say and she saw Dr Smith's smile fade.

'Are you all right, Rachel? I hope this pair of idiots didn't frighten the life out of you. I should have known better than to ask them to look out for you.'

'No, I'm fine. Really.' Her voice was a little too high and a little too bright but, although Dr Smith must have noticed that, he diplomatically chose not to comment.

'In that case, we'd better get down to business. There's a couple of things we need to sort out before we leave so if you'd like to come to the office...' He paused and glanced at the rucksack she was carrying.

'You can leave that here for now. We'll be loading up the personal luggage very shortly so it can go with the rest of the bags. There's nothing in it that shouldn't be there, I take it? We won't have problems with the Mexican authorities but some places we visit can be very sensitive, particularly about any recording equipment.'

'No. I went through the list you faxed me and made sure I didn't pack any cameras or tape recorders,' she replied, feeling easier now they were dealing with practicalities. It had been the shock of meeting Dr Smith for the first time which had caused that strange reaction, she assured herself. The earth most certainly hadn't moved!

The thought was less comforting than it should have been, however. Rachel was well aware that she didn't normally set much store by a person's appearance. As she followed Dr Smith through the warehouse, she promised herself that she would stop this nonsense immediately. She was there to do a job and she would focus on that from this point on.

'Sorry about the mess.' Dr Smith led the way into what was apparently his office. He scooped an armful of medical journals off a chair and dumped them on the floor. 'There never seems to be enough time to get everything done. Anyway, sit yourself down while I find your file. I know it's around here somewhere.'

Rachel sat, wondering faintly how long it would

take him to find her file amongst all the papers that were piled on his desk. It was an eclectic mix, bills of lading vying for space with glossy magazines, official-looking pink documents jumbled up with scraps of paper. Her gaze moved on while she took stock of the bulging filing cabinets, the cork-board covered with an inch-deep layer of sticky notes, and her heart sank. Such a total absence of order didn't bode well for the operation.

'Got it!'

Dr Smith shifted another load of journals off his chair and sat down. He quickly glanced at the crumpled sheet of paper he was holding and Rachel's lips snapped together when she realised it was her CV. She'd spent *hours* working on it and now it looked as though someone had been using it to make paper planes from.

'I see that you've been working on the children's ward for the last eight years. Why?'

Dr Smith shot the question at her and Rachel jumped. 'Because I enjoy the job,' she mumbled.

'And that's the only reason you haven't wanted to work anywhere else?'

'Yes. I can't think of a better one, can you?' she shot back because she didn't appreciate his tone. If he was implying there was something odd about her decision to remain in the post then she would prefer it if he came straight out and said so.

'No, I can't. However, we both know that people

carry on doing the same job for any number of reasons and not just because they enjoy it. I just want to be sure that you haven't stayed in the post because it's been the easy option, Rachel.'

He'd either read her mind or didn't believe in pulling his punches. Rachel suspected it was the latter but that suited her fine. If Dr Smith was happy to speak his mind then so was she.

'I don't take the easy option either in my work or in my personal life,' she told him coolly, her hazel eyes meeting his across the desk. A little spasm passed through her when she realised all of a sudden that his eyes were the most beautiful shade of green she had ever seen.

'Good. That's what I wanted to hear because there are no easy options in this line of work, Rachel. Everything you do from now on will be difficult and probably dangerous as well. We can't afford to have people along on this trip who think it's going to be a fun way to spend a couple of weeks. It won't be. I can promise you that.'

'I…I didn't apply to join the team because I thought it would be a way to have a free holiday,' she said hastily, struggling to rid her mind of all the extraneous thoughts that kept popping into it. What difference did it make if Dr Smith's eyes were green and beautiful and surrounded by the thickest, blackest lashes she'd ever seen? It didn't have any bearing on what they were discussing.

'Then that's another plus point. We get far too many people wanting to work for us who have no idea what the job really entails. We might fly all over the world but there's nothing glamorous about what we do, believe me.'

He swung his booted feet onto the desk, dislodging a heap of papers in the process. Rachel watched as they slithered to the floor, expecting that he would pick them up or curse or do *something*, but he never even glanced at them. He seemed completely oblivious to everything else, in fact, apart from her.

Rachel's heart began to pound because this wasn't what she'd expected when she'd set off that morning. She'd honestly believed that she was fully prepared for the task ahead because she'd gone through all the information that had been sent to her with the very finest-toothed comb. People who volunteered to work for Worlds Together had to be prepared to fly out to a disaster area at less than twenty-four hours' notice. They also had to accept that they did so at their own risk. Much had been made of the fact that the organisation was wholly non-political and that its sole aim was to provide skilled medical care wherever it was needed.

Rachel had read and digested every detail right down to the number of missions Worlds Together had been on since it had been founded five years ago—twenty-seven, if anyone had wanted to know—but she'd never allowed for one simple yet truly alarming fact: the way Dr John Shiloh Smith was looking at her—and how it made her feel.

Shiloh dredged up a smile but he knew he'd made a massive error of judgement by staring at Rachel like that. Letting her know that he found her attractive would only cause problems but he hadn't been able to help himself. The moment he'd seen her bells had started ringing and his pulse had started popping. He couldn't remember feeling like this since Sally had died.

He swung his feet off the desk because he couldn't sit there and deal with thoughts like that. Sally was dead and the life they'd had together had been filed away in the folder marked 'Past'. Maybe there was something about Rachel Hart that appealed to him but he was never going to act on it. She was just someone he would be working with for the next few weeks and so long as he was sure that she knew what she was letting herself in for he would have done his job.

'This is where we'll be working.' He took a map out of the filing cabinet and spread it on the desk, pointing to an area ringed with red ink. 'Mexico has suffered a number of earthquakes in the last few years but this is one of the worst they've experienced. The damage extends for hundreds of miles from the epicentre.'

'Do we have any idea of the number of casualties

we'll be dealing with?' Rachel asked as she bent forward to study the map.

'No. It's impossible to come up with a figure in this type of situation, but we're talking in thousands, not hundreds.' Shiloh took a deep breath because the sight of her pale, slender neck had made his groin suddenly tighten. She'd pinned her dark brown hair into a no-nonsense knot on the top of her head and he had the craziest urge to stand behind her and pull out all the pins…

'We'll be setting up a field hospital, I assume?'

She suddenly looked up and he just managed to stifle his groan when he saw her mouth purse as she waited for him to answer. It looked to all the world as though she was puckering her lips in readiness for his kiss and the thought almost blasted him into the next century.

'I…um…yes,' he muttered, struggling to bring his rioting hormones under control. 'Some of the team are already out there, getting everything ready for when we arrive. We'll be working under canvas because of the danger of further quakes, but we'll have all the usual facilities you'd expect—theatres, wards, treatment rooms, et cetera.' He tapped a blunt-tipped finger on the map, hoping it would help if he focused on all the minutiae of the operation. 'This will be our base right here.'

'Te-hua-t… Te-huat…' Rachel stumbled over the name and he laughed, trying to ignore the wave of tenderness that had washed through him when he'd heard her struggling with the unfamiliar syllables.

'It's an old Mayan Indian name and a real tongue-twister.' He managed to hold his smile, even imbue it with a degree of friendly teasing when she looked up. 'I doubt you'll need to phone for a taxi while you're out there so I wouldn't worry too much about getting it right.'

'That's a relief!'

She laughed as she sat back in her seat. Shiloh hastily removed his hand from the back of her chair but he wasn't quite quick enough to avoid making contact. Her right shoulder blade skimmed his knuckles and all of a sudden neurons started firing off messages to parts of his body he'd forgotten existed.

'That's basically all I can tell you for now,' he said, hurriedly returning to his seat. 'It's just a question of going out there and dealing with whatever we find. There's bound to have been a lot of children injured. They seem to come off worst in every disaster, which is why we were so pleased to receive your application last month.'

He was getting back into his stride now that he was safely ensconced behind his desk. It was just a question of mind over matter, he assured himself. Once he got control of his mind, nothing else would matter.

'That's what I was told at my interview.' Rachel sighed at the thought of all the children who might have been injured and Shiloh's pulse leapt when he felt the warmth of her breath flowing across the desk. Goose-bumps suddenly sprouted all over his body and he thanked heaven for the fact that the layers of clothing he was wearing hid them from sight.

'We've been desperate to find an experienced children's nurse to join the team,' he said hoarsely, struggling to get a grip on himself. 'We've advertised for volunteers a number of times but never had any luck until we received your letter.'

'I just happened to see your advertisement at a time when I was ready to try something different.' She shrugged when he looked at her quizzically. 'I've been suffering from empty-nest syndrome and this seemed the perfect way to get myself over it.'

'Empty-nest syndrome,' he repeated blankly before his mind suddenly joined up the dots.

'You mean that you have a family!' he exclaimed in dismay. Having children would not make this a suitable post for her. Not only would it take her away from them for weeks, but the work also involved considerable risks. The thought of having to explain to Rachel that it might be best if she didn't go was almost more than he could bear. Not only would she be dreadfully disappointed but he couldn't face the thought of leaving her behind when they'd only just met.

'Yes *and* no.' She laughed and somehow Shiloh

managed to drag himself back out of the pit of despair that had opened beneath his size-thirteen feet.

'And what's that supposed to mean? I really don't have time to play guessing games with you, Rachel,' he said with far more asperity than he'd intended. 'You either have children or you don't!'

'I'm sorry. I certainly wasn't trying to play games, Dr Smith. What I meant is that, although I don't have any children of my own, I've been responsible for bringing up my niece for the last few years. My sister was killed in a car accident, you see, and Bethany came to live with me afterwards.'

A wash of colour ran up her cheeks and Shiloh could have bitten off his tongue when he realised it was his fault that she looked so upset. 'I'm sorry to hear that,' he said gently, hoping to make amends for his clumsiness. 'Do I take it that your niece is old enough not to need you to look after her any longer?'

'Yes. Beth finished university last year and has taken time out to travel. She's in Australia at the moment and having a wonderful time from all accounts.' She shrugged but the clipped tone of her voice hinted that she hadn't forgiven him. 'That's why I felt it was time I got on and did something with my own life.'

'Well, it's certainly going to be different to what you're used to,' he replied, deciding it might be wiser to change the subject. Although he would have dearly loved to have found out more about Rachel, it really wasn't part of his remit.

'I know that but I'm sure I'll cope, Dr Smith. I wouldn't have volunteered to join the agency in the first place if I'd had any doubts about my capabilities.'

The frosty note in her voice stung just a little but Shiloh refused to let her see that it had had an effect on him. He tilted back his chair and regarded her levelly. 'And I'm sure that you will cope, too, Rachel. I wouldn't have agreed to take you on if I'd had any concerns about your suitability.'

One slender brow rose as she stared back at him. '*You* agreed to take me on? I thought it was the people who interviewed me who'd made the decision.'

'I vet everyone who joins this organisation,' he explained imperiously because he didn't appreciate having his word doubted. 'Nobody is taken on unless I say so. That goes for the people who clean the offices here right the way up to the surgical staff who work at the sharp end.'

'I see.' She treated him to a cool little smile then stared pointedly around the room. 'In that case may I suggest you get someone to double-check the next time you decide to hire any new staff. It would appear that some of the people you have working for you aren't quite up to the job!'

CHAPTER TWO

WHAT on *earth* had possessed her to say that?

When Rachel left the office a short time later she was still blushing. Admittedly, Dr Smith had taken her remark extremely well—laughing rather than putting her firmly in her place as he'd had every right to do—but that didn't make her feel any better about what had happened. She *never* spoke to people in that fashion and was known for her tact and diplomacy, yet that comment had trotted out before she'd had time to think about it. It just seemed to prove the strange effect Dr Smith had on her and it was unsettling to realise that she was going to have to deal with that as well as all the other new experiences that lay ahead.

'So you passed muster, did you?'

'Just about.' Rachel summoned a smile when Daniel came over to her. 'Though I don't suppose Dr Smith would have sent me packing at this late stage.'

'Don't you believe it! Shiloh wouldn't have thought twice about showing you the door if he'd decided you weren't up to the job.' Daniel tapped his nose and winked at her. 'I've seen it happen and it's not a pretty sight, believe me. Shiloh doesn't pull his punches.'

'Really?' Rachel couldn't hide her dismay as she realised how close she must have come to being thrown off the team. The thought of having to go back to Dalverston and tell all her friends that she'd been rejected was more than she could face and she gulped. 'Wh-when was the last time it happened, then?'

'Yesterday.' Daniel grinned when she gasped. 'It was a real shame, too, because she was *gorgeous*. Blonde hair, big blue eyes and even bigger...' He stopped and grimaced. 'Well, I'm sure you get the picture. Anyway, she turned up just after lunch in this snazzy little sports car with a stack of luggage piled in the back. Shiloh was out front, supervising the loading of some crates at the time, so Brian and I didn't get a chance to introduce ourselves. Before we knew what was happening, she was driving off again and not looking very pleased about it either.'

'Did Dr Smith say why he'd considered her to be unsuitable?' Rachel asked faintly.

'No, but that's Shiloh for you. He's a law unto himself and it's usually better not to ask too many questions in case you hear something you don't like. He doesn't suffer fools gladly and isn't backward when it comes to telling people about their shortcomings.'

Daniel gave her a wry smile then headed off down

an aisle. Rachel took a deep breath, wondering once
again what she was getting into. If Dr Smith was the
sort of boss who allowed his personal preferences to
influence his judgement then life could be very
fraught in the coming weeks…and yet he hadn't
given that impression while they'd been talking.
He'd seemed completely focused on the bigger picture and totally committed to the work that Worlds
Together did. She really couldn't imagine him being
petty for the sake of it.

It was all very puzzling and Rachel was glad to
put it out of her mind when Brian came to tell her
they would be leaving shortly. He took her to meet
the rest of the team, trotting out names and nicknames so fast that her head was spinning by the time
he'd finished. One of the women in the group must
have noticed her bewilderment because she laughed.

'Just ignore him, love. We're not all like him and
Daniel—completely off the wall and mad as hatters.'
She pretended to clip Brian round the ear when he
protested. 'Behave yourself! Poor Rachel will think
she's joined a lunatic asylum if you carry on like
that.'

'I was beginning to have my doubts,' Rachel
agreed, laughing. It was obvious the pair had a good
rapport and her spirits lifted because it was great to
see how well they got on together.

'And no wonder.' The woman got up and came
over to her. 'Let's start from the beginning again,

shall we? I'm June Morris and I'm also a nurse. My background is in surgery although I help out wherever I'm needed, as we all do. The rest of the nursing team consists of Katie Dexter over there, and Alison Woods, who's dozing in the corner…she's allowed to because she came here straight off night duty. Now, who have I missed? Oh, yes, Natalie. She flew out to Mexico yesterday with the advance party to get everything set up, so you'll meet her when we arrive.'

'Hi.' Rachel smiled at the other women. 'Nice to meet you.'

They smiled back then June carried on with the introductions. 'Steven Pierce is one of our anaesthetists and Daniel, believe it or not, is the other. Then there's David Preston, Liam Danson and Mike Rafferty who are all surgeons. That's it apart from Shiloh but you've met him already, I expect.'

'I have.' Rachel held her smile because she didn't want June to suspect there was anything wrong. However, as soon as she'd heard Dr Smith's name mentioned the strangest thing had happened. It was as though her blood had started fizzing, trillions of tiny bubbles forming and popping, and it was alarming when she had no idea why it was happening. It was a relief when Daniel appeared and announced that it was time for them to leave.

Rachel followed June out to the front of the warehouse where a minibus was waiting to ferry them to

the airport. She knew from her interview that they
would be travelling on scheduled flights and that the
seats were being provided free of charge by one of
the airlines who supported the organisation. Worlds
Together was a registered charity and depended entirely on donations for its funding.

They all piled onto the bus, everyone laughing and
joking as they set off for Heathrow. Dr Smith was
sitting up front beside the driver and seemed en-
grossed in some papers he was reading. Rachel sat
in the row behind with June and found herself study-
ing the back of his head as they drove away from
the docks. Although his hair had appeared to be
blond at first sight, she realised that it was in fact a
shade of mid-brown and that the top layers had been
bleached by repeated exposure to the sun. The sun
had also tanned his skin to a wonderful golden hue
which many fashion-conscious young women would
have paid a small fortune to emulate.

Rachel's gaze skimmed down the length of his
strong neck and a shiver ran through her when she
found herself wondering just how far his tan ex-
tended. Did it stretch right the way down his back
or did he cover himself up when he was outdoors to
protect his skin from damaging ultraviolet rays? She
couldn't imagine that he would bother taking any
precautions, funnily enough, which meant that his
chest would be tanned, too...

'Could you fill this in for me, Rachel? It will save time when we get to Mexico City.'

Rachel jumped when he suddenly turned round. A wash of colour ran up her face because it wasn't like her to start speculating about a man's body in such a fashion. She saw Dr Smith frown and rushed to forestall him because there was no way that she wanted to have to explain what was wrong. 'What is it?'

'Just a form stating that you are entering the country as part of a charitable aid mission.' He handed her the form but didn't release it for a moment as he studied her face. 'Are you all right? There's nothing worrying you, is there?'

'Of course not!' She almost snatched the paper off him and bent down to find a pen. She knew she'd put one in her bag before she'd set off for London that morning but could she find it?

'Here. Use this.'

His voice sounded gruff and a little impatient and Rachel's cheeks flamed with embarrassment. The last thing she wanted was him thinking that she was disorganised when it wasn't true. She took the pen with a murmur of thanks and set about filling in the form, adding her name, age, address and all the other details required from her. June glanced over at what she was doing and groaned.

'I sometimes think it would be easier if we had all that info·tattooed on our arms like a bar code.

Then we could be swiped in each time we entered a country!'

'Brilliant idea!' Rachel laughed, feeling better thanks to the other woman's unwitting intervention. She took a deep breath as she signed her name on the dotted line and handed back the form. She was getting all steamed up over nothing. Maybe she did seem to be behaving rather oddly but it was understandable when the situation was unlike anything she'd experienced before. Once she settled into the job then she would be fine. She would cope with the work no matter how difficult or dangerous it turned out to be because everyone else did. She would gain as much as possible from this trip and give as much back as she could to the people she treated.

As for Dr Smith, she would deal with him, too. Maybe he did have a strange effect on her but he was just a man like any other, made of flesh, blood and bone. There was no need to worry that she couldn't cope because he really couldn't affect her if she didn't let him.

By the time they landed at Mexico City, Shiloh was at his wits' end. Oh, the flight had been smooth enough and the food better than average, but the tension that had been building throughout the journey had reached danger level by that point. He didn't know how he'd managed to end up sitting next to

Rachel but he did know that it had been a test of endurance he could have done without.

Twelve hours of smelling the fragrance of her skin, of hearing her voice as she had spoken to June—who had been sitting across the aisle; twelve desperately long hours when he'd had to suffer the torment of feeling his body responding in a way it hadn't done in years had been too much for anyone to contend with. He'd hoped things might improve when she'd fallen asleep, and they had for a while, until her head had slipped sideways and ended up on his shoulder.

That had been the final straw, the one that had broken this particular camel's back. Shiloh hadn't felt even a smattering of guilt about waking her when he'd got up to go to the bathroom because he'd had no choice. It had been either that or…

He wasn't even going down that route!

They disembarked and were ferried through customs and immigration at a rate of knots thanks to their charity status. There was a truck waiting to collect them so all they had to do was ensure their baggage was on board and they were ready to leave. Shiloh made sure that he found a seat well away from Rachel and spent the next couple of hours bouncing over unpaved roads with his teeth gritted and his emotions just as firmly buttoned up. Whatever had happened on the plane was all in the past and he wouldn't allow it to interfere with the smooth running of the operation from here on.

The devastation from the earthquake was a shock even though most of the group had witnessed similar such scenes before. Silence fell as they travelled through the worst affected areas. Shiloh knew that everyone was thinking about what lay ahead and that it was his job to ensure they would be able to cope with the stress, but he also knew that people needed time to absorb what they were seeing. The reassurances could be saved till later when tiredness set in.

It was late afternoon when they drew up at the base camp. The tents had all been erected and everything was ready and waiting for them. Shiloh stood up to say a few words before they got off the truck.

'Most of you have seen this sort of thing before but still be careful. Don't push yourselves too hard. It's a lot to take in even for those of us who have far too much experience of working in the aftermath of a disaster like this. Be kind to yourselves as well as to the people you treat and you'll survive.'

His gaze moved to Rachel and his heart ached when he saw the shock on her face. He knew that he had to say something to her—a few words of reassurance—but it wasn't going to be easy to find the right note. He had to detach himself from what she might be feeling and it wouldn't be an easy thing to do when he felt her anguish almost as though it was his own.

The thought stunned him but he couldn't afford to let it get in the way as he drew her aside after everyone had left the truck. 'What I said just now about being kind to yourselves applies doubly to you, Rachel. You'll see some terrible sights in the coming days and you must be careful that you don't let them affect you too much.'

'How can you stop them affecting you?' she countered, her eyes huge and wounded as they lifted to his. 'There must have been hundreds of people killed by this earthquake and hundreds more injured!'

'That's what happens in a disaster,' he said gently. He put his hand under her elbow and led her away from the rest of the group, wanting to give her a few moments in private to collect herself.

'I know that...well, the rational bit of me knows it but the rest of me can't seem to take it all in.' She ran a hand over her face and Shiloh sucked in his breath when he saw the tears that were trembling on her lashes. If there'd been any way that he could have spared her this ordeal he would have done so, but there was nothing he could do except make sure that she was able to play her part on the team.

'It's all part and parcel of the job and you just have to deal with it,' he said flatly, using shock tactics because he knew that sympathy wouldn't work. If he did what he wanted to do—take her in his arms and promise her that he would make everything better—then he would be doing her a huge disservice even though it would have made him feel less like a bully.

'If you can't cope, Rachel, you may as well get right back in that truck and go home to England because you won't be a bit of use to us.'

She reared back as though he had slapped her and his heart ached afresh when he saw the disgust on her face. 'Thank you for your concern, Dr Smith. However, I assure you that I can cope with whatever you care to throw at me.'

'Good. Then let's not waste any more time discussing the matter.'

He strode back to the truck, rapping out orders in a tone that soon had everyone jumping to attention. Within minutes their bags had been unloaded and people were sorting out their sleeping arrangements. He saw June whisk Rachel away to the tent which she had commandeered for the nurses. It was on the edge of a clearing, shaded by some trees, and he smiled thinly because as usual June had found the best spot for her charges. At least he had the consolation of knowing that June would take care of Rachel, seeing as he couldn't.

'Shiloh!'

He spun round when he heard someone shouting him and saw Steven Pierce, one of their anaesthetists, waving to him. 'What's up?' he demanded, hurrying over to him.

'They've just dug a kid out of the ruins. He's in a bad way from all accounts—multiple fractures, internal bleeding—you name it and he's got it. He'll be arriving in about ten minutes' time so do you want to take it from here?'

'Yes, of course. Can you tell June that we need her then get everything set up?' Shiloh instructed as he headed for the largest of the tents which was home to the two operating theatres. 'I'll scrub up and be ready when he arrives.'

'June's already helping Liam,' Steven told him. 'They've got a woman who needs a Caesarean so they're taking her to Theatre.'

'What about Katie?' Shiloh suggested, not breaking stride.

'Natalie has commandeered her to help sort out the supplies. There was a hold-up at the airport last night so they only arrived an hour or so before we got here.'

'Alison?' Shiloh asked, his mouth compressing when Steven shook his head.

'Dead to the world. She's come straight off nights, don't forget.' Steven frowned. 'What's wrong with Rachel? I know she's been working in the children's wards for a long time but she mentioned that she has experience of working in Theatre.'

Shiloh hesitated even though Steven was right.

Rachel had done a stint in Theatre at the start of her career so she was more than qualified to assist him. It was just that he didn't want her getting upset again…

He shut off the thought. If Rachel couldn't cope, she shouldn't be there. Maybe this was the test she needed to prove to herself and to him that she was capable of doing the job?

'Fine. Tell Rachel to get scrubbed up, then, will you?'

He left Steven to deal with it and went into the tent, dropping the flap behind him and removing his boots before he entered the next section. Each theatre was really three tents, one leading into the other. The first section was the entrance and least sterile area, the next was where they changed and scrubbed up, and the third, largest area was the actual operating theatre. In there the air was purified by filters and everything was kept disinfected by the cleansing team. It wasn't perfect but it was as good as they could make it and Shiloh was proud of the fact that they'd never lost a patient through cross-contamination.

He shed his clothes then showered and changed into scrubs and set to, lathering his forearms with antibacterial soap and wielding a nailbrush with gusto. Rachel arrived just as he was finishing and he glanced at her, keeping it brief in case he gave away too much.

'Showers are through there and everything else you'll need is on the shelf. The facilities are communal, I'm afraid, because we don't have the space for separate male and female changing areas.'

'That's fine,' she said quietly, tossing her fleece jacket onto the bench. She sat down and stripped off her socks then reached for the hem of her sweater.

Shiloh turned back to face the sink, feeling his whole body suffuse with heat as she continued undressing. He couldn't actually see what she was doing and certainly didn't intend to look, but the small, intimate sounds—the rasp of a zip, the rustle of cotton—meant that his imagination was having a field day.

He gritted his teeth as the image of a semi-naked Rachel danced alluringly before his eyes. Her skin would be pearly and luminescent—her breasts, her midriff, her tummy and thighs. Of course, she wouldn't remove all her clothing with him there but there would be very little covering her, just a bra and a pair of panties, both probably plain and white because Rachel wasn't the kind of a woman who went in for bright colours or lace. She didn't need to enhance her beauty because it was more than sufficient. It was definitely enough for him!

He grabbed a towel off the shelf and dried his hands. He had no idea what Rachel was doing and didn't dare look at her to check. He found gloves and a mask then went into the inner sanctum and checked the instrument trolley. Scalpels, forceps, swabs, Rachel…

Shiloh swore softly and succinctly but it was better that he got it out of his system now rather than later. By the time Rachel appeared he was feeling a lot calmer, calm enough to be able to sound as though he hadn't a care in the world. Fat chance!

'All set, then?'

'Yes, thank you.'

As conversations went it wasn't the most earth-shattering he could remember but Shiloh derived a great deal of satisfaction from the fact that she sounded so composed. At least Rachel hadn't guessed what he'd been thinking and that counted for a lot. When Steven wheeled in their patient, he was ready to do his job and confident that Rachel would be able to do hers, too. As he bent over the small figure lying on the table, Shiloh thanked heaven that he'd managed to get a grip on himself. This was what was important—this child lying on the table, a young life in his hands—and he wouldn't let him down. Everything else was merely dross.

He saved lives and that's all that mattered, not his feelings or Rachel's or the lonely nights when he lay awake wishing that he had something to look forward to. He'd had plans once, lots of them, and they'd all been shattered when Sally had died. He'd sworn then that he wouldn't fall into the same trap again and he'd meant it, too. If he didn't hope for anything from life then he couldn't be hurt when it didn't happen.

It was the maxim he'd lived by for the last five years and it had served him well. There was no reason to change his mind because he'd met a woman who disturbed him. Falling in love might be wonderful but, by heaven, it hurt when things went wrong and he wasn't prepared to risk having his heart broken a second time!

CHAPTER THREE

'HIS spleen's ruptured. I'll need to remove it.'

Rachel slapped a scalpel into Shiloh's outstretched hand then glanced at the clock. They'd been in Theatre for almost two hours by then and there was still no end in sight. The child's injuries were so extensive that she couldn't believe he'd survived this long but he was clinging to life with a tenacity that defied all logic.

'Swab.'

She picked up a fresh swab with the forceps and carefully mopped away the blood, thanking heaven that she'd had the foresight to spend a few days in Theatre after she'd heard her application to join Worlds Together had been successful. It had been a while since she'd assisted during an operation and it had helped bolster up her confidence, although, thankfully, Shiloh was extremely precise about what he wanted done. He rapped out an order then left her to get on with it without any of the fuss so many surgeons made. Working with him had been a real pleasure as well as a learning curve because she'd never assisted anyone with his level of skill before.

She picked up a kidney dish and held it out so he

could drop the damaged organ into it. He nodded his thanks, his eyes never leaving the small figure lying on the table. 'I'll tie off the blood vessels then check to see what other damage I can find.'

Rachel deposited the dish on the trolley and picked up a wipe. Although the air-conditioning system was working it was still very hot in Theatre and she could see beads of perspiration gathering on his forehead. She carefully dabbed them away, trying to ignore the shiver that had run through her as she dropped the soiled wipe into the waste sack. She couldn't possibly have felt the heat of his skin through the double layer of gloves she was wearing so there was no point getting hung up on the idea. It was thoughts like that which would lead her to make a mistake and that was the last thing she wanted to happen when she needed to be on her mettle. If Dr Smith had asked her to assist so he could test her capabilities then she intended to put up a good showing.

They carried on, with Shiloh issuing orders and she responding to them while another hour passed. Rachel was just reaching the point where she was wondering how much longer it was going to take when Steven suddenly announced that the boy's blood pressure was dropping. Shiloh paused as he glanced towards the head of the operating table.

'Do you want me to stop?'

'I'm not sure…' Steven broke off and frantically

began resetting dials when one of the monitors started beeping a warning.

Rachel stood in silence and watched the anaesthetist pumping drugs into the small, inert body, drugs which, hopefully, would give the boy's heart the boost it needed. When the monitor screen went black apart from a single flat line she knew they'd failed and it was the worst feeling in the world, to know they hadn't been able to save the child despite all their efforts.

'That's it, then. I'm sorry. Thank you both. You did a first-rate job.'

Rachel looked up when Shiloh turned to her. There was a moment when their eyes met and her heart suddenly ached when she saw the anguish in his. In that instant, she realised how much he'd wanted to save the child and how much it had hurt him to fail. It made her feel suddenly ashamed because this had never been a test and had had nothing to do with her proving her worth. It was the child who'd mattered to Shiloh Smith, and if he'd had any doubts about her then it had been because he'd been concerned for his patient. Even though she knew that he wouldn't expect it, she would have to apologise and assure him that she understood why he'd been so brusque with her earlier.

They left Theatre a short time later but Rachel waited until Steven had gone to fetch a trolley before she said anything. Shiloh was removing his gown and he glanced round when she spoke.

'Can I have a word with you, Dr Smith?'

'Make it either Shiloh or John, please, Rachel. I don't care which you choose but I certainly can't see any need for us to stand on ceremony.'

'Oh, right, yes…um, Shiloh, then. I—I mean, that's what everyone else c-calls you.'

'It is. So, what did you want to say to me, then?'

He tossed his disposable gown into a waste sack then hauled the top of his scrubs over his head and dropped it into a laundry hamper. Rachel's heart lurched as she was suddenly treated to the sight of his torso in all its glory. Tanned skin seemed to stretch for acres across rippling muscles, the cushiony pad of light brown chest hair that formed an island in the centre the perfect place to lay her cheek…

Heat flooded through her and she looked away. She couldn't deal with ideas like that when she needed to have a calm and rational conversation with him. 'I just wanted to apologise for the way I behaved earlier on. I understand now why you were so concerned about me doing this job.'

'You do?'

There was a note in his voice that sent a shiver skittering down her spine and she almost looked at him. It was just the thought of what might greet her that kept her staring at the tent wall. Was that the sound of cotton rustling? she wondered, her ears positively twitching when they detected the very faintest of noises. She bit her lip because the only cotton item Shiloh had been wearing the last time she'd looked had been a pair of trousers and there was no *way* that she wanted to see what he had on now!

'Yes.' Her voice bore a strong resemblance to that of a famous cartoon mouse but Rachel battled on. It was either carry on talking or turn round and look at him and the latter wasn't an option. 'Y-you wanted to be sure that I was mentally prepared to help these people, Shiloh. I realise that now. It wasn't anything personal but concern for your patients which prompted you to speak to me so…well, so sharply before.'

'I wish I could claim that was true, Rachel, but I'd be lying, I'm afraid.'

The rueful comment caught her completely off guard and she swung round. There was a moment when her eyes drank in the long, muscular legs, the narrow hips modestly covered by a pair of black shorts, and then she managed to drag them up to his face. Rachel's heart began to thump so hard that its drumming beat sounded like a herd of stampeding cattle but there wasn't a thing she could do about it. A thumping heart was the least of her worries compared to the way Shiloh was looking at her now, his eyes so filled with emotion that she could barely breathe.

'It had nothing to do with our patients, Rachel. I know damned well that you can do this job. It was *you* I was worried about, how *you* would cope with all the awful sights you'll see in the next few weeks.'

He ran a trembling hand over his face and she started to tremble as well when she saw how distraught he suddenly looked. Shiloh looked like a man on the very edge and it was so out of line with everything she'd learned about him that it shook her.

'You were worried about me? About me and my feelings?'

'Yes. Crazy, isn't it? I mean, we've only just met and I certainly don't go in for this kind of thing...'

'What kind of thing?' she interjected because she desperately needed to know what he meant.

'This, of course. The way I feel about you. It's absolutely ridiculous!'

His eyes glimmered with sudden anger but it didn't mask all the other emotions she could see in them as well. Rachel bit her lip but there was no way she could resist asking the question even though she had no idea what she was going to do about the answer.

'And how *do* you feel about me?'

'I'm not sure how to describe it. I thought at first that it was merely physical attraction and that was bad enough, of course, but now I'm not sure what it is.'

'Can't you make a guess?' she prompted then put

her hands over her mouth in horror when she realised what she'd said.

'I could, but it wouldn't be right to speculate.' His smile was suddenly wry as he came towards her. Rachel felt her breath catch when he stopped right in front of her. He was so close now that she could have reached out her hand and touched him…

She put her hands behind her back because she really couldn't deal with anything more right now. 'Why would it be wrong to speculate if it turned out to be true?'

'Because it would give you a completely false idea about what might happen,' he said deeply, his voice rumbling up from the very depths of his chest. 'Whatever I may or may not feel for you, Rachel, it doesn't matter. It can't do because I'll never act on it. I know what I have to do with my life and there's no room in it for a relationship.'

He touched her then, just lightly on the cheek, but it felt as though he'd laid her down on the floor and made love to her. Rachel gasped when she felt the rush of sensations that flooded her body. Oh, she knew how desire felt. She'd experienced the first heady rush, the heat, the fever but it had always been within the boundaries of a committed relationship and an act of love. She couldn't understand how the touch of this man's hand could have caused such havoc so it was a relief when Shiloh stepped back because she didn't think she could have stood there much longer without responding.

'I've felt this way only once before, Rachel, and although it was wonderful while it lasted, it was hell when it ended. I swore that I would never put myself in the same position again and I meant it.'

He smiled at her, such a gentle, tender smile that her heart overflowed with warmth. 'There's something about you that makes me want things I never thought I'd want again but I won't take the risk of getting hurt a second time. If I've embarrassed you by saying all this then I apologise, but it's usually best to know what you're dealing with, I always find.'

'I'm not embarrassed,' she whispered because it was true and that thought shocked her all over again. This man had just declared that he was attracted to her and she had accepted it without question. But was it really so surprising? Wasn't it simply a measure of the man he was that he could make such an admission and that she would believe him?

Her heart began to race all over again and she knew that she had to leave before she did something they would both regret. Shiloh had been honest about his feelings and she wouldn't do anything to make the situation any more difficult for him...

Only she couldn't help herself.

She laid her hand on his cheek, left it there for the space of a single heartbeat, then turned and fled.

Night had fallen and nobody saw her running out of the tent. She paused just long enough to strip off her gown and toss it into a bio-hazard sack by the entrance then made her way to the nurses' quarters. It was dinner-time and there was nobody there so she sat on her bed and thought about what had happened and what Shiloh had said. Tears stung her eyes but she knuckled them away.

She wouldn't cry for something she'd never had! she told herself firmly, then realised that she wasn't crying for herself but for Shiloh. Pain lanced her heart because even though she had no idea what had happened to him in the past, she did know how awful it must be for him to have chosen to live his life without love.

Shiloh stabbed his fork into a chunk of steak and popped it into his mouth. He chewed and swallowed, hoping that he wouldn't throw up. He speared a lump of potato next but the thought of actually forcing it down his throat was just too much. Leaving his plate on the table, he got up and went to the door.

It was almost midnight and everywhere was quiet apart from the drone of machinery in the distance where the diggers were working. The local people were working round the clock to dig their families out of the ruins of the town. There'd been a steady influx of injured brought to the camp all evening long but it had tailed off a short while back which was why he'd decided to take a break. Mike Rafferty had offered to take the graveyard shift but Shiloh had preferred to do it himself. It was better to stay busy than think about what had happened with Rachel.

'The food's not that bad, is it?'

He glanced up when he recognised Natalie Palmer's voice, summoning a smile as he stepped aside to let her into the mess tent. He and Natalie had trained at the same university although she'd changed her mind halfway through her course and had gone into nursing instead of finishing her degree in medicine. They'd kept in touch afterwards and it had been Natalie who'd encouraged him to set up Worlds Together after Sally had died.

'The food's fine but I'm just not hungry.'

'I heard about the boy, Shiloh. Bad luck.'

'You win some and you lose some,' he replied lightly, but she wasn't fooled.

'And it hurts like hell every time you lose one.' She smiled up at him. 'So now we've got that out of the way, why don't you tell me what's really wrong? I know you're upset about the boy—who wouldn't be? But there's something else worrying you, isn't there?'

'Is there?' he countered, turning to stare across the clearing. There was a light on in the nurses' tent and his heart thumped as he found himself wondering if Rachel was awake, thinking about what had happened earlier. He must have been mad to tell her all that, mad or desperate, and he hadn't decided yet which it was.

'I'd say so but, then, who am I to judge what goes on inside a man's head?' she replied ironically.

'Don't tell me—you and Mike have had another difference of opinion?'

'How did you guess?' She huffed out a sigh. 'He is *so* pig-headed! I mean, it isn't my fault that my parents happen to be loaded. If it isn't a problem for me then I can't see why it should be a problem for him.'

'Ah, the course of true love. It never did run smoothly.'

'Except for you and Sally. You two were such a shining example that I doubt anyone could live up to your standards.' She laughed. 'Why, I can't remember you two ever disagreeing. You were just made for each other...'

'Excuse me.'

They both swung round when a quiet voice suddenly interrupted their conversation. Shiloh felt his stomach sink when he saw Rachel standing outside the tent. Had she overheard what Natalie had said? he wondered sickly, although there was no reason in the world why he should feel embarrassed if she had heard that remark about him and Sally.

He moved out of the way, sucking in his breath when her shoulder accidentally brushed his chest as she came into the tent. 'Are you hungry?' he asked because he had to say something to stop himself grabbing hold of her. A wave of longing so intense swept through him that he gripped hold of the tent pole with a white-knuckled hand. Things were getting out of control and he had to stop what was happening...

Only it wasn't going to be easy, he realised when she looked up and their eyes met. He was already in far deeper than he'd intended. Oh, hell!

'I just needed a drink of water,' she explained in such a neutral tone that it shouldn't have caused any reaction at all.

Shiloh gripped the tent pole so hard that it creaked when he felt his body quicken with desire. His eyes glazed with despair because there was no way that prosaic little statement could have been mistaken for a come-on yet it had had that effect on him.

'There's fresh water in the cooler,' he explained grimly, pointing towards the far corner of the tent with his free hand.

'Yes, I know, but thanks anyway.'

She treated him to a tight little smile then headed for the cooler. Shiloh's eyes followed her, savouring the gentle sway of her hips, the straightness of her back, the tilt of her head. She was wearing combat trousers in a sludgy shade of green and an old T-shirt that probably couldn't remember seeing any better days yet she still looked fabulous—slim, womanly, sexy...

He groaned.

'Coffee, I think.' Natalie grabbed his hand and briskly prised his fingers away from the tent pole. She marched him across the tent and sat him down in a chair. 'Sit there and I'll fetch it.'

'Oh, but—'

'No buts, Smith. Do as you're told,' she ordered, glaring at him.

Shiloh subsided into the seat as she went to fetch the coffee. Natalie was the sweetest-natured woman in the world—until she was aroused. It was no wonder that she and Rafferty were having problems getting it together because she could be equally pig-headed. It needed a degree of compromise to make a relationship work, not that he was in a position to offer advice, of course. He and Sally had dovetailed their lives together so perfectly that their marriage had been seamless from the outset. They hadn't needed to work at getting it right because it had been purely magical. How could he ever hope to find that kind of rapport again?

His gaze skimmed helplessly to the far corner and his heart began to thump all over again as he watched Rachel fill a beaker with water. The tap on the cooler was loose and he saw her leap back in surprise when a shower of water suddenly spurted out. She put the beaker on the table then dabbed at the wet patch that had formed on the front of her T-shirt and Shiloh groaned again.

Was she *deliberately* trying to torment him by running her hand over her breasts like that? Even from this distance he could see how her nipples had tightened after their drenching in cold water and his wayward body set off down what was becoming an increasingly familiar route. He hastily crossed his legs when he felt the muscles in his groin tighten but there was no way he could prevent the inevitable from happening, not unless he indulged in a cold shower as well…

Now, there was a thought. Him and Rachel stark naked together under a stream of cool water…

'Coffee. Black and sweet, just how you like it, so drink up.' Natalie plonked a mug in front of him and he jumped. She gave him an old-fashioned look and to Shiloh's mortification he actually blushed. 'My, my, I never thought I'd live to see the day,' she said silkily, sitting down.

'If you have something to say then why not just say it? I'm not in the mood for your cryptic remarks,' he growled because he hated what was happening to him, hated it and wanted it to stop. The fact that he couldn't make his body obey him only made matters worse.

'OK. I never thought I'd live to see the day when you were having the hots for a woman.' Natalie smiled sweetly at him. 'That *is* what's bothering you, isn't it? I mean, the signs all point towards it.'

'What signs? You're talking rubbish as usual,' he snapped, but she wasn't deterred.

'Am I? So you aren't lusting after the lovely Rachel? Dear me, I must have got it all wrong. Sorry.' She sipped her coffee then smiled blithely at him. 'It must be the time of the month or something.'

Shiloh rolled his eyes. There was no point trying to pretend with Natalie because she knew him too well. 'All right, so maybe I do like Rachel but we both know I'm not going to do anything about it. No, correction, we *all* know that I'm not going to do anything about it,' he amended belligerently.

'So you've told her how you feel, have you? Well, that's something I certainly didn't expect to hear.' Natalie put her cup on the table and looked at him. 'Sally wouldn't have wanted you to spend the rest of your life grieving for her, Shiloh.'

'I know that!'

He pushed back his chair because there was only so much he could deal with in any given day and he'd already surpassed his limit. His heart suddenly lurched when Rachel murmured good night as she passed them but he couldn't weaken, wouldn't ever put himself through the heartache he'd been through before.

'It's an early start in the morning so don't forget to set your alarm,' he warned her in his most imperious tone, the one he usually reserved for any students who thought it might be fun to muck around during one of his lectures. They never tried it again, though, after he'd set them straight.

'It's already set. Don't worry. I won't be late.'

Her smile was the sweetest thing he'd seen in years and he just stood there and basked in its glow after Rachel left. It was only when Natalie delicately coughed that he realised what he was doing. He snatched up his mug of coffee and glared at her.

'Don't you dare say anything!'

'Of course not,' she replied sweetly, not even bothering to hide her smile.

Shiloh muttered something ungentlemanly which he would have to apologise for in the morning and made a speedy exit. He stomped back to his tent and flung himself down on the rickety little cot. What was that saying about tomorrow being another day? Well, he hoped it was true, prayed that tomorrow would bring him some peace of mind, but he doubted it. Whilst Rachel was around peace of mind—and body—were going to be in short supply!

CHAPTER FOUR

'INCOMING wounded! TC wants you in Theatre like yesterday, Hot-lips!'

Rachel looked up when Brian Parker stuck his head inside the tent and relayed the message. There'd been another delivery that morning so she and Natalie were in the supplies tent, sorting it all out. It had been three days since she'd arrived in Mexico and she seemed to have slipped into the routine with surprisingly little trouble. The work was familiar even if the conditions weren't, and the fact that everyone was so helpful had soon eased her into the flow. Apart from that small hiccup on her first day, in fact, everything had been fine.

'OK, I've worked out that you're Hot-lips but who's TC?' she asked, steering her mind away from the dangerous topic of Shiloh Smith. So maybe that snippet of conversation she'd overheard the other night had been haunting her ever since but it was none of her business what had gone on between him and the unknown Sally. There was no point getting all worked up either because he'd admitted that he was attracted to her, not when he'd made it perfectly clear that he wasn't going to do anything about it…

'Rafferty.'

Natalie dumped a stack of boxes onto the shelf and Rachel blinked. She summoned a smile but it was alarming to realise how easily her thoughts kept returning to Shiloh. He'd been nothing less than courteous towards her in the last few days and if he hadn't confessed how he felt then she would never have guessed. However, there was no way she could forget what had happened even if he'd been able to do so.

'I see. So what does it stand for?' she asked, trying to ignore the niggling little pain that had wormed its way into her heart. If Shiloh had decided that the best way to handle the situation was by ignoring it then there was nothing she could do about it.

'Top Cat. Highly appropriate, too, in my opinion. He's definitely bossy enough to warrant it!'

'Hmm, do I detect a *hint* of animosity in that statement?' Rachel asked, grinning when Natalie rolled her eyes.

'Not just a hint, more like a cartload!' Natalie deposited another pile of boxes on the shelf and glared at them as though they were to blame for her ill temper. 'He has to be the most stubborn man I've ever met. If they handed out medals for being pig-headed, Michael James Rafferty would earn himself gold every time!'

'Far be it from me to interrupt you, Sister Palmer, when you are busy assassinating my character but we do happen to have a patient on his way to Theatre.'

They both swung round and Rachel grimaced when she saw Mike Rafferty and Shiloh standing outside the tent. She swallowed her giggle when Shiloh's left eyelid slowly lowered as he winked at her.

'And far be it from me to keep you waiting, sir!' Natalie retorted, standing to attention and saluting. 'Would you like me to crawl to Theatre on my hands and knees to atone for my sins, or would it be sufficient if I followed you at a distance suited to my lowly rank?'

'Do whatever the hell you like. You always do!'

A moment's silence followed the other couple's departure. Rachel sighed as she picked up the clipboard. 'I hope they both calm down before they reach Theatre.'

'Don't worry. They're far too professional to let their personal feelings spill over into their work.' Shiloh poked his head inside the tent and groaned when he saw the cartons. 'What a mess! I take it we had another delivery?'

'Yes. It arrived this morning—mainly cleaning stuff for the Theatres plus some dressings,' she explained, feeling a shiver tickle her spine. He was still wearing his theatre greens and she was instantly transported back to that first night. The sight of his muscular physique was one memory she would most definitely be taking home with her when she left Mexico.

She swung round and desperately began counting boxes as images of Shiloh flickered before her eyes. Concentrate, Rachel, she told herself sternly. Focus on all the boring tasks that you could do in your sleep…or could do if you didn't spend your nights dreaming about Shiloh. Her pen gouged a lump out of the flimsy document attached to the clipboard and she swore under her breath then looked up when Shiloh laughed.

'I don't blame you, Rachel. It would make a saint swear.'

'It would?' she squeaked, wondering how he'd guessed what had been going on inside her head.

'Of course.' He took the clipboard from her then gently removed the pen from her nerveless fingers as well. 'It's frustrating to have to spend your time checking supplies when you want to get on with the job, isn't it? Why don't we do it together and that way it will be finished in half the time?'

'Oh, right, I see. Thanks.'

Rachel spun round and began counting boxes again, sending up a heartfelt prayer that he would never discover what she'd really been thinking about. 'Sixteen,' she told him in a tight little voice because she felt such a fool.

'Sixteen what?'

'Oh, size six dressings. Sorry.'

'No need to apologise. What's next?'

Rachel bent to drag a crate into the centre of the floor. She jumped when a large hand suddenly appeared before her.

'That's far too heavy for you to move. Let me do it.' He quickly moved the packing case into place then looked round. 'We need something to prise off the lid…'

'Use this.' She handed him the crowbar which Natalie had commandeered from the back of one of the trucks and he chuckled.

'Trust you nurses to have everything to hand!'

She laughed dutifully but it was hard to batten down her emotions as she watched him slide the metal bar beneath the lid. Muscles in his forearms flexed as he levered it off and set it aside, making a mockery of the length of time it had taken her and Natalie to open the first crate. It had taken them ages to prise the lid off the wretched thing but Shiloh had done it in the mere blink of an eye.

'What?'

'Pardon?' She jumped, feeling the ready colour run up her face when she found him staring at her.

'I was just wondering what you were thinking,' he explained in a tone that added all sorts of meanings to an otherwise innocuous sentence. 'You were miles away just now.'

'Was I? Sorry…' She stopped and grimaced. 'There I go again! I was just remembering how long it took me and Natalie to open the other crate. We couldn't get the wretched lid off and yet it took you just a couple of seconds and—hey presto—you had it open.'

'One of the few advantages of being this large,' he observed lightly, bending to lift the cardboard cartons out of the crate.

'Only a *few* advantages?' she queried, placing one of the boxes on the table. It was another collection of dressings of various shapes and sizes so she reached for the clipboard and started ticking them off the list.

'Uh-huh. Folk say that size doesn't matter but, believe me, it can be a real handicap at times. I mean, you try looking graceful on a dance floor when you have size thirteen feet.' He shook his head so that a blond lock fell onto his forehead. 'I suppose that's why you never see a six-foot-four ballet dancer. His feet would be too big to fit into those tiny satin pumps.'

Rachel burst out laughing because the thought was too ridiculous for words. 'I'm sure you're right. OK, fair enough, so it obviously limited your career choices but you must have found it useful to be so tall in other areas of your life. I mean, you can see over everyone's head at a football match or a concert, and you'd hardly ever need a ladder to reach the top shelf…'

'Oh, you may mock, young lady, but life isn't easy

for those of us who are vertically enhanced.' He handed her another carton and his smile was so warm that she almost forgot what she was supposed to be doing. 'You try finding trousers long enough to fit and shirts with sleeves that reach past your elbows and *then* you'll understand how hard it is!'

'It…it must be difficult at times,' she conceded, putting the box on the table and hastily checking its contents so she could gain a few desperately needed seconds of breathing space but it was a waste of time.

When had a smile ever made her feel as though she was melting? she wondered dizzily. When had it made her stomach knot and her breath get all tangled up? When had just a smile made her feel as though she was fully and completely alive?

Never! the answer came back. Not once in all her thirty-two years had a smile had such an effect and it was alarming to admit it. She'd thought she'd been in love before, firmly believed that she'd met the man she had wanted to spend the rest of her life with, yet she'd never once felt the way she felt when Shiloh smiled at her.

Her hands shook as she stacked the box on the shelf because she hadn't been prepared for something like this to happen. She'd volunteered for this trip because she'd wanted to help people. The fact that it would also lift her life out of the doldrums had been a bonus, of course. Yet all of a sudden Rachel found herself standing on the brink of an experience unlike anything she'd known before and she didn't know what to do. Should she tell Shiloh how she felt or should she keep it to herself?

Shiloh wasn't sure what Rachel was thinking as he watched myriad expressions cross her face. She looked shocked, scared and elated all mixed up together and the need to find out what was going on inside her head was so great that he almost gave in and asked her...almost but not quite.

He gritted his teeth as he bent and hauled another carton out of the crate. It was frustrating to know that he had to put a limit on what they could discuss when he wanted to explore her mind almost as much as he wanted to explore her beautiful body. He handed her the box so she could check it off the list but it was a relief when June appeared.

'Rachel, can you take a look at a little girl who's just been brought in? Her parents are with her and they're desperately worried. She wasn't injured in the earthquake and David's examined her but he's at a loss to know what's wrong. He wants you to have a look and see if you can come up with any ideas.'

'Of course.' Rachel hurried to the entrance then paused to glance back. 'I'll be back as soon as I can.'

'There's no rush,' Shiloh assured her, hoping she couldn't tell how relieved he felt. Another couple of seconds and he'd have given in and asked her to tell him what was wrong and that certainly wouldn't have helped the situation. He treated her to what he hoped was a purely friendly smile. 'I'll carry on with the unpacking until you get back.'

'Thanks.' She returned his smile then left the tent, and the moment she'd gone it felt as though the light had gone out and the sun was no longer shining.

Shiloh breathed deeply as he returned to the task of unloading the supplies but it wasn't possible to shut out the thoughts that were whizzing round his head. Every time he spoke to Rachel this feeling of attraction grew stronger. He hoped he'd be able to control it but he wasn't sure if he had enough strength. And yet if he gave in then he would be breaking every rule that had made his life bearable these past five years. Talk about being stuck between a rock and a hard place!

'Shh, *pequeña.*'

Rachel brushed the hair off the child's hot little face. Five-year-old Maria-Luz Hernandez was extremely ill and her parents had every reason to be worried about her. David Preston had run every test he could think of to find out what was wrong with the child but, as he'd openly admitted, he was a surgeon, not a physician, and it could be something he hadn't thought of.

Rachel turned to the child's parents, hoping they might be able to shed some light on the situation. Maria-Luz's temperature was 39 degrees centigrade and she had a rash on her arms and legs. She'd been vomiting and was suffering from diarrhoea as well. Her stats were down and there were signs that her kidneys weren't functioning properly. A high white-cell count indicated there was an infection present.

'How long has your daughter been ill?' Rachel asked, waiting while the interpreter translated her question.

'*Dos días*,' Maria-Luz's mother replied anxiously.

'Two days.' Rachel nodded. 'And has she had a fever for all that time?'

'*No sé.*'

Señora Hernandez broke into a flood of rapid Spanish. Rachel listened while the interpreter explained that Maria-Luz had been a little off colour to begin with but they'd thought she'd had a chill. After the earthquake had struck, they'd been so busy trying to make sure that Maria and her brothers were safe that they'd not realised her condition had worsened.

'It's understandable,' Rachel assured the couple. She turned back the sheet and carefully examined the child again, rolling her onto her side and frowning when she saw the scar on the child's upper left abdomen. 'Ask them if Maria-Luz has had her spleen removed,' she instructed.

'Yes, last year,' the interpreter explained after a brief conversation. 'She was knocked down by a car and the surgeon had to remove it.'

'Which means that she's far more susceptible to

infection,' Rachel observed thoughtfully. She glanced at David. 'There's a possibility that it could be meningitis, of course. The rash is right, although she doesn't seem to have any problems with the light and her neck isn't stiff.'

'I thought of that but didn't want to do a lumbar puncture until you'd taken a look. I've put her on broad-spec antibiotics to be on the safe side, though.'

'Good.' Rachel rolled the little girl onto her back again. She frowned when she suddenly noticed a mark a couple of inches above the child's right ankle. Bending closer she could see that it was a bite mark, probably from a dog, and her heart sank. Rabies hadn't been eradicated in Mexico and she dreaded to think that it might be the cause of Maria-Luz's illness even though the child's symptoms weren't indicative of the disease.

'Did you notice this bite on her leg?' she asked, drawing David's attention to it.

'No, I didn't,' he exclaimed in dismay, obviously following her train of thought. 'I'll get a blood test done and check it out.'

'Let's hope it isn't what we think,' Rachel said softly. She glanced round when someone came into the tent and felt her heart squeeze in an extra beat when she saw Shiloh. It was all she could do to concentrate as he came to join them.

'Any ideas yet?' he asked, glancing from her to David.

'Yes, and nothing good either,' David said glumly, indicating the mark on the little girl's leg.

Señora Hernandez broke into another torrent of Spanish, flinging up her arms and shaking her head and they all turned expectantly towards the interpreter.

'She says that it was her neighbour's dog and that it's the third time this month that it's bitten one of her children,' he explained. 'She's told the neighbour that if it does it again she will shoot it!'

'Have the other children shown any symptoms?' Shiloh put in quickly, and Rachel smiled because she'd been about to ask that very question. Two minds with but a single thought, she thought, then briskly put the idea out of her head because it was far too emotive.

'No, the other children are fine. It's just Maria-Luz who is ill,' the answer came back.

'Interesting.' Shiloh frowned as he looked at the little girl. 'You'd think if it was something she'd caught from the dog then the other kids would have shown symptoms as well.'

'Not necessarily. Maria has had her spleen removed so that will have made her more susceptible to infection,' Rachel explained quickly.

'It certainly would,' he agreed. 'Well, the one good thing is that I doubt if it's rabies. That rash isn't one of the symptoms you'd expect to find in a case of rabies. However, it's spot on if she's been infected with capnocytophaga and suffering from catastrophic sepsis as a result. The bacteria are present in the mouths of all dogs and cats, although most people aren't infected if they're bitten. But someone like this little one—whose immune system has already been compromised through losing her spleen—would be a prime candidate.'

'So you think that's what's wrong with her?' Rachel put in eagerly, because it sounded so much better than what she'd feared.

'It's a strong possibility although we'll need to run some tests to confirm it. Unfortunately, it takes time to do the blood cultures but we'll treat her with benzyl penicillin and metronidazole as well as the cefotaxime. That should sort things out with a bit of luck but she's a very sick little girl and she's going to need a lot of careful nursing if she's to pull through.'

'That's my department,' Rachel assured him, then turned to the interpreter and asked him to explain to Maria-Luz's parents that they would need to keep her in.

Señora Hernandez seemed relieved by the news and thanked her warmly, holding Rachel's hand and repeating over and over in broken English, 'Thank you, thank you.'

'I'll take good care of her,' Rachel told her with a lump in her throat, and the mother seemed to understand without needing any translation.

They moved Maria-Luz to the ward and made her comfortable then gave the whole Hernandez family something to eat and drink which resulted in another round of heartfelt thanks. Rachel stayed with Maria-Luz for the rest of the day, wanting to be on hand if her condition worsened. There were a dozen other patients in there as well, most of them people who'd been pulled out of the ruins of the town, so she was kept busy and stayed long after her shift should have finished. There was so much to do and everyone was so grateful that it made her weariness seem very trivial. It was only when Shiloh appeared with a cloth-wrapped bundle in his hands that she glanced at her watch and discovered how late it was.

'You've done more than your fair share today, Rachel,' he announced as he came over to the desk. He pulled back the end of the tea-towel so she could see the thick tortilla inside and grinned at her. 'How do you fancy getting away from here for an impromptu picnic?'

'That was absolutely delicious!'

Shiloh laughed when he heard the contentment in Rachel's voice. Parting the folds of the tea-towel, he found the last smidgen of tortilla and offered it to her. 'Want the last bit?'

'No, you have it.' She daintily licked her fingers as she lent back against the tree trunk. 'I am absolutely stuffed to the gills!'

'Oh, very ladylike, Miss Hart,' he teased, popping the last chunk of the savoury omelette into his mouth.

'Don't care,' she retorted, sticking out her tongue at him. 'Who wants to be all prim and proper in the middle of the jungle, anyway?'

'Very true,' Shiloh agreed dryly, looking around. He'd borrowed one of the trucks and had driven them away from the camp to have their picnic. If they'd stayed on site he knew they would have ended up working through dinner and he'd been anxious that Rachel should take a break after her long day. One of the locals had told him about the old Mayan ruins a couple of miles outside the town so he'd headed there. Although the main pyramid had fallen into ruin, it was easy to imagine how imposing it must have been.

'It must have been an amazing sight when it was built,' Rachel observed softly, and he sighed. Had it been a lucky coincidence she'd said that or because there was a spiritual bond between them as well as a physical one?

'Have you ever seen Chichen Itza?' he asked, desperately trying to drive that idea out of his head. It was bad enough that he was so deeply attracted to her without making matters worse.

'Only in photographs. Tom and I did talk about having a holiday in Cancun at one point. We were hoping to visit the ruins while we were there but our plans fell through in the end.'

'Tom?' he queried hoarsely because the thought of there being some other man in Rachel's life was more than he could bear. He couldn't believe that he hadn't considered the idea before. She was so beautiful that she must have men queuing up for her attention.

'Oh, just someone I knew a while back,' she said lightly enough, but he heard the faint undercurrent in her voice and guessed that this Tom fellow had played a key role in her life at one time.

A searing pain lanced his heart and he had to breathe deeply before it eased. Frankly, he couldn't believe that he was jealous at the thought of Rachel having a relationship with a man but it was true. He'd always thought he was above that sort of thing because he certainly hadn't felt like this when he and Sally had been together.

He stood up abruptly, deeply uncomfortable with the thought that he'd never been jealous about Sally's past life but he was jealous about Rachel's. Bundling the tea-towel into a ball, he tossed it into the truck then turned to suggest that it was time they headed back. Rachel was still sitting with her back against the tree but there was an expression on her face now that made his heart suddenly race. It was obvious that something was bothering her and Shiloh knew he wouldn't rest until he'd found out what was wrong.

He sat down again, waiting until she glanced his

way before he spoke. 'What's the matter? I can tell something is worrying you.'

'I'm fine,' she denied, and he sighed.

'You're not fine so tell me what's wrong. Please.' He heard her take a quick breath and felt his stomach muscles bunch because he had a nasty feeling he was going to regret asking that question.

'What happened to Sally? I know it's got absolutely nothing to do with me, Shiloh, but I'd still like to know.' She shrugged but he could tell how important this was to her. 'I overheard what Natalie said the other night about you and Sally being the perfect couple. Was she your wife?'

'Yes.'

'So, what happened?'

Shiloh stared at his hands. There was no way he could avoid telling her the truth and no reason to do so but it wasn't easy to talk about what had happened even now. 'Sally died.'

'Died?'

He heard the shock in Rachel's voice and grimaced because he hadn't wanted to upset her. 'Yes. She was driving home one night after work when she crashed her car. The police think she probably swerved to avoid another vehicle. There were skid marks on the tarmac and a witness reported seeing another car driving off at the time of the accident but nobody came forward when the police appealed for information.'

'I had no idea…' She broke off.

'There's no reason why you should have known,' he pointed out.

'Maybe not but I wish I hadn't asked you now,' she admitted in a sad little voice that tugged at his heartstrings.

'You wanted to know the truth and it's understandable. Anyway, it isn't as though it's a secret. A lot of the folk working on the team know what happened.' He laughed ruefully. 'Some of them even helped pick up the pieces afterwards. Suffice to say that I fell apart.'

'I can't imagine what you must have gone through. Breaking up with someone you love is bad enough but this… It goes way beyond anything else, doesn't it?'

'Yes,' he agreed because he wouldn't lie to her about something so important. 'It felt as though my world had come to an end when Sally died. I couldn't seem to take it in. People kept telling me that she was dead but in here…' he tapped his head '…she was still alive and I just didn't believe them.'

'Oh, Shiloh!' She laid her hand on his and he felt the hot sting of tears burning his eyelids. It was all he could do to continue but now that he'd started he had a sudden need to tell her everything, all the things that he'd told nobody else.

He turned his hand over and gripped hers, holding onto it as all the pain came flooding back. 'We used to have a favourite spot on the Downs where we'd go when we had any time off work. Sally was a doctor, too, you see, so free time was always at a premium. Anyway, I remember going there one day about a month after it had happened and kneeling on the ground and begging her to come back. I was so angry that she'd left me that I even cursed her. I wanted my life back, all the plans we'd made, all the dreams we'd had. I didn't want to face the future without her. I honestly didn't think I could keep going without her.'

'But you did,' Rachel said softly when he paused. 'You kept going because you knew it was what Sally would have wanted you to do.'

'Yes.' He dragged in a ragged breath, struggling with the emotions that were bubbling inside him. He hadn't allowed himself to experience them for a long time and it was scary to feel their power again after all the time that had elapsed. 'Natalie suggested that I set up Worlds Together. It was something the three of us had often talked about doing and she knew that I needed something to focus on that would keep me sane. She was right, too, because it gave me a purpose in life, a reason to keep going until, gradually, I found that I could cope.'

He shrugged. 'Seeing how other people learn to deal with the disasters that befall them also helped. I felt less…well, less *alone*, if you can understand what I mean by that.'

'I think I do,' she said in a choked voice.

Shiloh's heart turned over when he saw the tears that were streaming down her face. 'Oh, hell! I am *so* sorry, sweetheart. I never meant to upset you like this.'

'You haven't,' she began, then laughed shakily. 'Not much point trying to be polite by lying, is there?'

'None at all,' he said gravely, feeling in his pocket and handing her a wad of tissues. He waited while she blew her nose and dried her eyes. 'All right now?'

'I think so.' She dredged up a smile and it was that which proved to be his undoing. He didn't even pause to think of the mistake he might be making as he drew her into his arms and held her tightly. Rachel's bravery had touched his heart more than anything had touched it for a long, long time.

His hand slid beneath her chin so he could tilt her face up to receive his kiss. Her cheek was velvety soft and damp from her tears when his lips brushed against it on their way to her mouth and he shuddered. The feel of her skin was the most potent aphrodisiac, one guaranteed to set his senses alight, and his body responded immediately.

Blood rushed to his head, blurring his sight so that Rachel's face seemed to shimmer before him in a pool of light and he knew that he had to touch her. He ran his knuckles down her cheek, let them follow the line of her jaw then brought them back to stop by her mouth and all the time his heart was pounding harder and harder and his body was begging for more. Her lips suddenly parted on a sigh and it was the softest yet the most erotic sound he'd ever heard so that he groaned loudly, painfully, and in anguish.

'Have you any idea how much I want you, Rachel?'

'Yes.' Her hand slid down his body and came to rest on the hardness of his arousal as she looked him straight in the eyes. 'I can feel what this is doing to you, Shiloh, and all we've done is kiss. Crazy, isn't it? How can you want someone so much that your body burns? How can you long to feel their hands on you so desperately that you would be willing to give up ten years of your life just to have your wish come true? It doesn't make sense to me so maybe you can explain it.'

'I wish I could. I wish I could make sense of what's happening but it's the same for me as it is for you.'

He broke off because he needed to savour that thought, relish it, store it away for the days ahead when he wouldn't have Rachel in his arms. The thought sent a chill through him and he shivered, felt her do the same but knew it was for a different reason. Rachel didn't have the same doubts he had, she didn't understand there was a limit on what he could give her, and it struck him once again how wrong it was to let this happen, how cruel it would be to promise her the moon and not be able to deliver.

'We must stop—' he began, but she didn't let him finish, just put her mouth to his and kissed him with the kind of passion he'd been dreaming about for the past three days and nights.

Shiloh groaned when he felt her lips fitting themselves to his so perfectly that they might have been made from the same mould. Her mouth was so soft and sweet and hungry—so very hungry!—that he couldn't push her away. He drew her into his arms and held her against his heart as passion flashed between them—red-hot, brilliant, searing their senses, imprinting itself onto their minds and spirits. And in that second he knew that, no matter what regrets they might have later, they would never regret this moment. It was what they had been born for; it was their time and they would never forget it until the day they both died.

CHAPTER FIVE

'So HOW did it go last night? Did you and Shiloh have a good time?'

Rachel was checking Maria-Luz's obs the following morning when Natalie came to find her. She'd managed to avoid any awkward questions by making sure she had been up and dressed before the other nurses had woken up. She'd also skipped breakfast, contenting herself with a cup of coffee that one of the orderlies had fetched for her. Maybe it was silly to be so wary but she wanted to be sure that she'd got used to the idea of her and Shiloh's new relationship before anyone else found out.

Her heart skipped several beats at the thought of how their relationship had changed last night. He'd been the most tender lover after their first greedy coupling. Their hunger had been so great at first that they'd not been able to hold back as passion had carried them away. But the second time had been different, gentler, more loving…

'Rachel?'

She jumped, summoning a smile when she saw the way the other woman was looking at her. 'It was fine. We went to the Mayan ruins. I don't know if you've seen them yet but they're quite spectacular, especially at night when the moon rises…' She stopped and swallowed because the memory of Shiloh's body all dappled with moonlight was a lot to contend with.

Natalie sighed. 'I know it hasn't anything to do with me, Rachel, but you will be careful, won't you? I wouldn't like to see Shiloh get hurt. He's been through such a lot.'

'You mean Sally?' Rachel shrugged when she saw Natalie's surprise. 'Shiloh told me what had happened to her and how it had affected him. It must have been awful for him.'

'It was. At one point I thought we were going to lose him, too, because he was such a mess.' An expression of pain crossed Natalie's face before she smiled. 'Thankfully, it's all in the past now but he's still…well, *vulnerable*, if that doesn't sound ridiculous.'

'It doesn't sound ridiculous at all. I understand why you're concerned but I would never do anything to hurt him,' she assured her, then broke off when June came into the tent.

'What are you two plotting?' June demanded as she came over to them. 'If you're trying to bribe Rachel to work in Theatre with your beloved then you'd better bribe me as well so I don't tell her what a demon he can be!'

'He's not my *beloved* and you can tell him I said that if he asks!' Natalie retorted.

They all laughed but Rachel was relieved the subject had been changed. Although she hadn't been offended by Natalie's remarks, it wasn't easy to discuss her relationship with Shiloh when it was still so new and fresh.

'You and Rafferty need your heads knocked together,' June said tartly. 'For two intelligent people, you sure are making a mess of your lives. He loves you and you love him so what's the problem?'

'Money.' Natalie smiled tightly. 'I have it and Rafferty doesn't. End of story.' She sketched them a wave then headed out of the tent.

Rachel watched her leave and frowned. 'Is that true? Are they really fighting over money?'

'Apparently.' June sighed. 'Natalie's family is loaded. Ever heard of Palmer Pharmaceuticals?'

'Of course I have. You don't mean that Natalie is related to them, do you?' she exclaimed in amazement.

'Oh, yes, I do. Her father is head of the company and as the adored only child, Natalie stands to inherit the lot. Rafferty can't handle the thought of her being so rich, especially when he comes from a really poor background.' June grimaced. 'Men and their pride, eh.'

'I had no idea. Natalie is just so…well, so *normal*.'

'She is. She certainly doesn't try to lord it over everyone. She's a wonderful friend and especially to

Shiloh. Mind you, we all look out for Shiloh whenever we can.'

Rachel sighed when she heard the warning note in
the older woman's voice. 'If that was a subtle way
of telling me to be careful I don't hurt him then I
shall, June.'

'Good. Right, what's next on the agenda? I believe
we've got an American team joining us today—a
couple of physicians plus another nurse. Should
lighten the load a bit.'

Rachel was happy to concentrate on work after
that but she knew that June and Natalie probably
weren't the only ones who were worried about her
and Shiloh. Not that they need have any concerns
about the way she was going to treat him. The last
thing she wanted was to hurt him.

It was another hectic morning, not helped by the
fact that they had several new admissions. They were
fast reaching saturation point but, thankfully, the authorities had reopened the main highway so some of
their patients would be transferred to a local hospital
very shortly. Rachel got the new patients settled and
wrote up their charts as best she could when there
were so few details available. The earthquake had
torn apart whole families and she couldn't imagine
how awful it must be for those who were left behind.
Although the rescue teams were still working in the
ruins, the chances of them pulling anyone else out
alive were decreasing by the hour.

Maria-Luz's condition started to deteriorate shortly before midday. Rachel had been checking her obs at half-hourly intervals and she was alarmed when she discovered that the child's urine output had dropped. She left one of the orderlies in charge and went for help, heading straight to Theatre because that's where she'd find Shiloh. He was in the scrub room when she tracked him down, stripped to the waist because he was scrubbing up between ops. Rachel stopped dead when she saw him and the memory of the previous night hit her afresh. He suddenly looked round and she saw the most beautiful smile light up his face.

'Hi! Were you looking for me, by any chance?'

'Yes.' She cleared her throat, struggled to keep her tone even, then ruined it all by grinning inanely at him. 'You are just the man I need, in fact.'

'It must be my lucky day,' he murmured wickedly, making her blush.

'Stop that!' she ordered, trying her best to stay focused.

'Yes, ma'am. Sorry, ma'am!' he responded, laughing as he reached for a towel and dried his hands. He tossed it into the sink then came over to her and Rachel gulped when she suddenly found her nose level with the thatch of hair on his chest. Her pulse seemed to be going crazy, popping and pounding, and her breathing sounded like the wheezing of an old steam engine. When Shiloh tilted her chin so that he could look into her eyes, she almost collapsed into a heap at his feet.

'So what can I do for you this morning, Sister Hart?' he asked, his deep voice sounding all warm and buttery, and Rachel groaned.

'You really shouldn't ask questions like that after last night!'

'Shouldn't I?' he whispered as he bent and kissed her.

'No. You never know what kind of an answer you'll get.'

'Maybe not but it could be fun finding out,' he murmured, his mouth brushing tormentingly against hers.

'You are a real tease, Shiloh Smith. And to think that everyone is worried about me hurting you! If anyone's at risk here then it's me.'

'What do you mean?' He drew back and Rachel felt a chill run through her when she saw the frown on his face.

'Both Natalie and June have made it plain that they're worried in case I might…well, hurt you,' she admitted. She looked him in the eyes because she didn't want there to be any mistake about what she was saying. 'I told them what I'll tell you, that the last thing I want to do is to hurt you in any way.'

'I'm sorry.' He let her go abruptly and stepped back. 'They really shouldn't have said anything to you. I'll have a word with them.'

'It isn't a problem,' she assured him. 'And I understand why they're concerned. They care a great deal about you, Shiloh, and in their shoes I'd feel exactly the same way.'

She took a deep breath but she had to ask the question even though she wasn't sure that she would like the answer. There was just something about the way Shiloh was looking at her…

'What happened last night wasn't planned and it took us both by surprise. I don't regret it but what about you? Are you sorry it happened, Shiloh?'

'No.'

Shiloh returned Rachel's delighted smile although his conscience was giving him gyp. Maybe he didn't *regret* what had happened but he wasn't completely happy about it either. He could accept that the first time they'd made love they'd been swept away by their feelings, but the second time…what had happened then?

Once for passion but twice for love, a small voice taunted, and the words seemed to hammer into his brain like nails being hammered into a coffin.

'And that's why I'd like you to take a look at her.'

Shiloh dragged his mind back from such dangerous thoughts and hurriedly pieced together what Rachel had said. 'Give me a minute to put some clothes on and I'll be right with you,' he told her gruffly.

'Thanks.' She rewarded him with a smile then hurried away.

Shiloh popped his head into Theatre and quickly explained that he needed to check on a patient in the hospital bay. Fortunately, Daniel hadn't started anaesthetising their next case so it wouldn't cause too many problems if he was away for a few minutes. It took him just a few seconds to pop on some clothes, not much longer to make his way to the hospital tent. Rachel was standing beside the little girl's bed when he arrived, holding Maria-Luz's hand, and Shiloh knew that the image would remain with him long after the moment had passed.

Rachel's concern for their patients was just something else about her that he found so attractive. Didn't she have any faults at all, he wondered as he made his way to the child's bed, nothing that would bring his feet back to solid ground and make their parting easier to bear when the time came, as it would? Apparently not and it made the situation all the more stressful and heart-rending—all those things he'd sworn he wouldn't allow it to become so that it was difficult to appear the concerned professional rather than the abject lover.

'How is she doing?' he asked, determined to focus on the child's problems rather than his own. He'd battened down his emotions for five long years and he wasn't about to let them run riot now.

'Not good. Her blood pressure is down—not by

very much but it's not what it should be,' she told him, her thoughts obviously centred on Maria-Luz, which was a blessing.

'We'll up her fluids and I'll write her up for diuretics to increase her urine output but it's only a temporary measure, I'm afraid. Kidney failure is common in this situation and she's probably going to need dialysis if she's to have a chance of pulling through.'

'Can we do that here?' Rachel asked worriedly.

'No, we don't have the equipment. I doubt if the local hospital has it either which means that she'll need to be transferred to some place that can deal with it.' He glanced at her, felt his heart ache when he saw the concern on her face and made himself take a mental if not a physical step back. 'I'll see if I can find a hospital willing to treat her. Our best hope is either Cancun or Puerto Vallarta where they have hospitals catering for the tourist trade.'

'Will they do it for free, though?' she asked, and Shiloh couldn't stop himself reaching out and squeezing her hand when he heard the anxiety in her voice.

'Maybe. But if they won't then we'll find a way round it somehow or other. We have some extremely generous sponsors who are usually prepared to help in a case like this. Don't worry, Rachel. I'll work something out.'

'I know you'll give it your best shot, Shiloh, and

that's all anyone can ask,' she told him, and there was so much warmth in her voice that all thoughts of behaving sensibly fled.

He drew her into the alcove that had been screened off for the use of the nursing staff and kissed her hungrily. Rachel's eyes were still closed when he drew back so he had a moment to study her rapt expression before her lids rose. His heart began to thump when he saw the expression in her eyes, all the tenderness and warmth.

'I'll have to go,' he said roughly because it was just too difficult to sound calm at that moment. 'I've a patient waiting in Theatre.'

'And I'd better get back to work before the boss starts complaining.'

Shiloh smiled but he made his way back to Theatre as though pursued by demons and maybe he was, too. As he tersely informed Daniel that he needed to make a few phone calls, he could feel the sickness building inside him. All of a sudden it felt as though his life was hurtling out of control and it had been years since he'd felt this way—five to put an exact figure on it. Five long years when he had struggled against the pain and heartache, the overwhelming sense of loss. He'd found stability eventually, at least earned himself a measure of peace even if happiness had eluded him, but it felt as though he was back right to where he'd started—his life in tatters, his emotions in turmoil, his body in torment—and it was too much to deal with.

He couldn't fall in love with Rachel because he couldn't bear it! He wouldn't allow her to fall in love with him either, because that would be almost as bad. He didn't want to be responsible for her happiness. He'd been in that situation before and he couldn't live with the fear that one day it might all go wrong as it had for him and Sally. He would rather be alone for the rest of his days than put up with that kind of misery again.

The fluids and diuretics had helped to stabilise Maria-Luz but Rachel knew it was only a temporary reprieve. She carried on with her work, praying that Shiloh would find a hospital willing to treat the child. The whole Hernandez family had now taken up residence close to the camp site, setting up a rickety shelter made from sticks and paper on the perimeter. Rachel was introduced to Maria-Luz's brothers as well as her aunts, uncles and cousins at various stages throughout the day. The whole family was so grateful that it became embarrassing having to deal with their repeated thanks. Señora Hernandez took it upon herself to show her gratitude in her own way and Rachel was deeply touched when the woman brought her a beautiful white blouse embroidered with the traditional patterns used by the women in the area.

'It is absolutely lovely, *Señora*, but I really can't accept it,' she protested, knowing how little the family had left after the earthquake.

'*Sí, sí.*' Señora Hernandez pushed the blouse into Rachel's hands. '*Es un regalo para usted, señorita.*'

'*Gracias.*' Rachel gave in when she realised that it would cause offence if she didn't accept the gift. She held up the blouse so she could admire it. '*Es muy hermoso,*' she declared, dredging up some school Spanish.

The whole family applauded loudly before they went away to sit with Maria-Luz. They were obviously delighted their gift had been so well received although Rachel still felt guilty about taking it and said so when June came over to see what had been happening.

'I hate taking things off people when they have so little for themselves,' she explained, showing June the blouse.

'I know, but folk like to thank us and you did the right thing by accepting it.' June sighed as she fingered the rich embroidery around the neck of the blouse. 'I wish I was young enough to wear it. It will look fabulous on you, Rachel.'

'Think so?' She held it against her while she tried to see her reflection in the door of the metal storage cupboard. When a figure suddenly appeared behind her she spun round and felt her heart leap when she saw Shiloh.

'Señora Hernandez insisted on giving me this,' she told him in a breathy little voice that made June chuckle before she tactfully excused herself.

'It's beautiful,' he said, his eyes lingering on the soft swell of her breasts beneath the fine white cotton for a moment before he noisily cleared his throat. 'I just came to let you know that I've managed to find a bed for Maria-Luz at a hospital in Cancun. They have a fully equipped renal unit and as luck would have it they happen to have a bed free at the moment.'

'That's wonderful!' she exclaimed, doing her best to follow his lead by concentrating on work. 'How will we get her there, though? I'm not sure how far we are from the coast but it must be an awfully long way by road.'

'It is, which is why she'll be going by helicopter. The American team has agreed that their pilot can fly Maria to the hospital on his way back to Miami.'

'Even better. Won't someone need to go with her?'

'Yes. That's what I need to sort out. You can go if you want to, Rachel. Or I can ask Natalie. She might be glad of a break after the spat she and Rafferty had this morning.'

'Don't tell me they've had another argument?' She sighed when he nodded. 'I do wish they'd sort out their problems, don't you?'

'Yes, but it's up to them to find a compromise. So

what do you want to do? D'you fancy a trip to Miami?'

'It's tempting but how will I get back here?' she asked slowly.

'You won't.' He took a deep breath and she saw his face close up as though he was deliberately trying to batten down his emotions. 'If you go to Miami then you'll have to catch a flight back to England in the morning.' He shrugged. 'I couldn't justify the expense of flying you back here when we'll probably be leaving at the end of the week.'

'I see. And is that what you want me to do, Shiloh—fly home to England?' she asked, unable to keep the hurt out of her voice.

'It would solve a lot of problems...'

'I'm not interested in solving problems!' she retorted. Last night had been so wonderful even though she'd never planned on it happening. She didn't really know what it meant because she hadn't allowed herself to think about *why* she'd slept with Shiloh apart from the obvious reason—that she'd wanted him so much. She'd certainly never been the kind of woman who slept around. Maybe it was an old-fashioned view but she didn't believe in sex without love so at some point she would have to examine her reasons but not now, not when she needed to know how Shiloh felt about her leaving.

'I don't care about solving problems,' she repeated

more quietly. 'I asked you if you wanted me to leave?'

'No. I can't think of anything I want less than to lose you when I've only just found you,' he ground out.

'Good.' Rachel laughed shakily when she heard the passion in his voice. 'Because I don't want to leave you either. Not when I've just found you, too.'

'Rachel, I...' He stopped and shook his head. 'I really don't know what to say. How can I tell you that you'd be better off going home when I feel sick at the thought of you leaving?'

'Then don't say anything. When I was small my mother used to tell me that if a thing didn't feel right then I shouldn't do it,' she said tenderly because it was hard to see this big, powerful man at the mercy of his own emotions.

'And it's as easy as that, is it? Every problem can be solved simply by relying on your feelings?'

His scepticism stung but she smiled because she sensed he was only trying to protect himself. 'No, it's not that simple but it's a place to start.' She took his hand and held it tightly, willing him to believe her. 'I won't hurt you, Shiloh. Trust me and trust your instincts as well.'

'I know you mean that but sometimes people don't have a choice about what happens.' His other hand cupped her face and his eyes were filled with pain. 'Nobody can guarantee a *happy ever after*, Rachel, and that's what scares me. I couldn't go through what I went through before.'

'I understand. Really I do,' she told him, but her heart was aching because there was so little she could say to reassure him. She let go of his hand and picked up the blouse, folding it carefully back into its tissue paper because she sensed they both needed some time alone to think. 'I'd better put this away before it gets dirty.'

'And I'd better tell Natalie that she'll be going to Miami.'

Rachel glanced up when she heard the rawness in his voice. He looked like a man in torment and the thought that she might be responsible for putting him through such agony was more than she could stand. 'Shiloh—'

'No.' He put his finger on her mouth, stemming the words before she could utter them. 'I want you to stay, Rachel. That's all that needs to be said at the moment.'

Tears filled her eyes but she didn't say anything else because she didn't want to upset him. She went back to the nurses' quarters and carefully stowed the blouse away in her bag then washed her hands and face because it meant that Shiloh would have gone by the time she went back. Maybe she was getting too worked up about all this. Maybe all they needed to do was to get used to the idea of them being to-gether…

She sank onto the narrow cot when the sheer futility of that hope hit her. There was no point pretending they had a future. All they had was last night and what might happen tonight and all the other nights until they went back to England then it would end. She'd never envisaged having an affair but that was what this was and she had to accept it. It was either that or take up that offer to leave and that would be unbearable for both of them. So long as Shiloh didn't get hurt then she would cope with whatever had to be done.

Rachel went back to the hospital. She was just about to go inside when the sound of a helicopter made her look round. She watched as it landed in the clearing then hurried inside. The American team had arrived which meant that Maria-Luz would need to be prepared for the transfer.

Shiloh had explained to the Hernandez family what was happening so Rachel was able to get the child ready without it causing any problems. Natalie arrived just as she'd finished updating Maria-Luz's notes and told her that Señora Hernandez would be going to Miami as well because the pilot had agreed to take an extra passenger. Apparently, the *señora* had relatives living in Cancun and she would stay with them so she could visit her daughter in hospital.

Rachel kissed the child's cheek then moved away from the bed when she heard footsteps approaching. She looked round, expecting it to be Shiloh, and so it was, but he had someone with him, another man who looked very familiar. Rachel gasped when the newcomer stepped forward.

'Rachel! I don't believe it. What on earth are *you* doing here?'

'Tom?' she whispered incredulously. 'Tom!'

'In the flesh. At least you haven't forgotten me.' He laughed as he swept her into his arms and hugged her. 'This has to be the best thing that's happened to me in ages!'

CHAPTER SIX

'PERHAPS we could leave the reunions until later. I'd like to get this child to hospital as soon as possible, if you wouldn't mind.'

Shiloh heard the bite in his voice but he certainly didn't intend to apologise for it. He glowered as the other man reluctantly released Rachel. He had no idea who the fellow was but he took exception to the way he'd manhandled her.

'Thank you. Now, if you'd all like to help we'll get her onto the trolley. On my count—one, two, three.'

Maria-Luz was quickly moved onto the wheeled stretcher. Shiloh waited while Rachel checked the drip was still firmly anchored to the child's arm. She nodded as she unhooked the bag of saline and drugs from the stand but he was acutely aware that she'd avoided looking directly at him. Embarrassment because of the spectacle her friend had made of her? Shiloh wondered. Or guilt because of what had happened between them last night?

Tension knotted his guts as he wheeled the stretcher out to the helicopter. The American team was unloading their belongings and they looked round when they heard him approaching.

'So this is the little one who's going for a ride, is it?' a pretty, young, fair-haired woman remarked, bending to look at the child. She glanced up and Shiloh saw her smile widen when her eyes alighted on him. 'Hi! I'm Jolene Martin and you must be Shiloh Smith. I've heard *so* much about you.'

Shiloh merely nodded because he couldn't have cared less if she found him attractive. Rachel was speaking to that Tom fellow again and he was more concerned about what they were saying. He swung round, struggling not to betray any emotion as he addressed her.

'Did you remember her notes?'

'Natalie has them,' Rachel told him, a touch of colour blooming in her cheeks.

'They're fully up to date, I hope?' he demanded, wondering if the blush had been for his benefit or Tom's. A frown creased his brow because the name seemed to ring a bell. When had he last heard it mentioned?

'Of course.'

There was a snap in Rachel's voice this time but Shiloh swallowed the apology that sprang to his lips. She was obviously annoyed because he'd apparently doubted her competence but it was tough. She should have kept her mind on the job instead of spending it gossiping with an old flame.

Shiloh felt his stomach sink as it hit him when he'd heard the name Tom mentioned. It had been last night while he and Rachel had been chatting before.... Well, *before*. Was this Tom the same man she'd told him about, the man with whom she'd planned to go on holiday at one point? He guessed it was true and the thought was more than he could stand only he had to because he didn't have a choice. It was either that or thump Tom on the nose and he could just imagine the uproar that would cause!

They loaded Maria-Luz into the helicopter then he helped Señora Hernandez aboard. Natalie handed her bag to the pilot then came to say goodbye. She hugged him and Shiloh could see the concern on her face when she stepped back.

'Be careful, won't you, Shiloh? I like Rachel a lot but I don't want you getting hurt.'

'I'll be fine,' he assured her with far more confidence than he felt. 'I'm more worried about you and that crazy Irishman. Have you two sorted things out yet?'

'Hell will freeze over before Rafferty gives in and sees sense,' she told him with a laugh that didn't disguise the pain in her eyes.

'I'm so sorry, Nat.' He hugged her then sighed. 'We're a right pair. Me with my hang-ups and you stuck with loving a guy who can't see past the pound signs.'

'Nobody said life was going to be easy,' she told him, making a determined effort to be cheerful.

The pilot came to tell them he was ready to leave

so Shiloh helped her on board. Maria-Luz had been made comfortable and Señora Hernandez was strapped into her seat. Shiloh waved to them as the doors were closed then moved out of the way when the pilot started the engine. He made his way to the edge of the clearing and stood there while the helicopter took off. The American team had gone to find their sleeping quarters and get settled in before they started work. There was no sign of Rachel but Shiloh deliberately closed his mind to the thought of where she might be and with whom. There was no point going down that route. No point at all.

Rachel went back to the hospital but she was still reeling from the shock of seeing Tom again. It had been six years since she'd seen him last and she'd never in her wildest dreams expected him to turn up like that. Alison Woods came to relieve her a short time later and it was obvious that news of their meeting had spread like wildfire through the camp.

'I hear you had a surprise today,' Alison said cheerfully. She was a sensible young woman in her twenties, happily engaged to a doctor at the hospital where she worked and looking forward to their wedding which was scheduled to take place the following month.

'I certainly did,' Rachel replied airily because she didn't want people making too much of what had happened. Her heart missed a beat because she had no idea what Shiloh must have thought about the way Tom had hugged her so enthusiastically.

'Tom and I used to work together at Dalverston General. He accepted a place on the overseas exchange programme so we lost touch. It was a real shock to see him again here, I can tell you.'

'Oh, I see! So he was just a colleague, was he?' Alison chuckled. 'Bang goes Katie's theory that you two were an item. I think she was hoping for some kind of *grand reunion* but she's going to be disappointed from the sound of it. She'll have to stick to getting her thrills from her romance novels instead of the real thing!'

Rachel laughed although she couldn't help feeling a little uncomfortable. She and Tom had been a lot more than colleagues six years ago and it was alarming to know that other people had picked up on that fact. It made her see how urgent it was that she spoke to Shiloh. She couldn't bear to think of him getting the wrong idea into his head, too.

She left the hospital and went straight to Theatre but he was already operating. There was no point waiting when she had no idea how long he would be so she went to the mess tent and had something to eat then wandered outside. She was off duty until the evening and normally would have spent the time resting but she felt too restless to sit in her tent and read. Maybe she would take a walk until Shiloh had finished. She had to make sure he understood there was nothing left between her and Tom…

Was that right, though? Was she *sure* that she was over Tom?

The thought brought her to a halt. Rachel could feel her heart pounding as she considered it. She'd loved Tom Hartley very much at one time and had hoped to spend her life with him but a series of unforeseen events had forced them to split up. It had been a painful episode in her life and it had taken her a long time to get over it. Could she be absolutely sure that she still didn't feel something for him?

Rachel bit her lip because it was impossible to answer those questions. She didn't know how she really felt about Tom and it scared her to admit it because of the repercussions it might cause. The last thing she wanted to do was to hurt Shiloh but she might not be able to avoid it if she still cared for Tom.

'That's it. I'll put in a drain and close up. With a bit of luck, he should make it.'

Shiloh flexed his aching shoulders then set about the final stages of the operation. The young man he'd been operating on had suffered extensive abdominal injuries but Shiloh was fairly confident that he would recover. He was the last patient on a very long list and Shiloh was looking forward to a well-deserved break. However, the benefit of working such long hours was the fact that he'd been able to forget about Rachel for a while. Now, as he put the final stitch into the wound, all his earlier fears came rushing back.

'Thanks, everyone. That was a good day's work,' he said, struggling to remain focused, no easy task when his mind was trying out a variety of possible scenarios. Was Rachel with Tom at this very minute? Were they busily catching up and discovering the old attraction was still very much alive? He'd seen the way that Tom fellow had hugged her—who hadn't?—so maybe he was wasting no time, convincing her that he wanted her back. After all, Rachel hadn't exactly fought him off and if that wasn't a sign of her feelings then, by heaven, he didn't know what was!

By the time Shiloh left Theatre he was in such a state that he could barely think straight. He dumped his theatre clothes into the various receptacles then showered and dressed. It was early evening and the light was fading fast as it did in that part of the world. When he and Rachel had arrived at the Mayan ruins last night it had been daylight but within an hour the moon had come up.

Pain rippled along his nerves as he suddenly recalled how beautiful she'd looked, lying naked in his arms. All he'd had was that one night to enjoy her beauty and it wasn't enough. The thought of some other man being   with   her   was   more   than   he   could bear but he had to be realistic. If Tom was the man she'd loved once upon a time then there was a strong chance she still harboured feelings for him. He couldn't and wouldn't stand in the way of her happiness when he had nothing to offer her.

Dinner that night was once again tortillas but the food tasted like sawdust now, not manna from heaven. Shiloh ate because he needed fuel to keep functioning but every mouthful threatened to choke him. He kept remembering Rachel's enjoyment of the simple meal last night, how she had licked her fingers after finishing the last mouthful…

He pushed back his chair because he couldn't sit there and think about what had happened otherwise he'd drive himself crazy. He had to talk to Rachel and get her to tell him the truth about Tom. If it was bad news then he preferred to meet it head on.

She wasn't in her tent and Katie, who was lying on her bed reading one of her favourite romance novels, had no idea where she'd gone. Shiloh tried all the usual places he would have expected to find her but each time drew a blank. The Americans were sitting outside their tent, playing cards, and the one good thing was that Tom was with them which meant he wasn't with Rachel. In the end, he left the camp and made his way to the river because people would start talking if he kept wandering around like a lost soul. And that was where he found her, sitting on the river bank in the moonlight.

Shiloh stopped and took a deep breath. He wasn't sure how he felt at that moment because it was all such a jumble—relief mixed up with fear, joy wrapped around with sadness. He felt so many conflicting emotions when he looked at Rachel and the fact that he felt anything at all simply proved how deeply committed he was.

The idea sent a chill right through his soul so that it was hard to smile when she looked round and saw him, but, then, she wasn't smiling either. Shiloh's heart seemed to be playing ping-pong with his ribs when he realised how solemn she looked. He couldn't begin to disguise his alarm as he hurried over and hunkered down in front of her.

'Are you all right, sweetheart?'

'Yes.' She laid her palm against his cheek and he gulped because the touch of her hand was almost too much after what he'd been through that afternoon. 'How about you?'

'Better…now,' he whispered, unable to lie.

'Oh, Shiloh!' She wrapped her arms around his neck and kissed him like a mother kissing a frightened child—with comfort and compassion—and his masculinity was immediately affronted. He wasn't a child but a man with a man's feelings and a man's desires!

He put his arms around her and took charge, kissing her with hunger and passion and every other emotion that exists between a man and a woman. Her sigh was like music to his ears, making him feel ten feet tall and ready to face any challenge. He grinned because the thought was so basic that he could scarcely believe it and she looked at him with a small frown pleating her brows.

'What are you smiling about?'

'Because I was just wondering if there was the odd dinosaur I could kill and bring back to the cave for supper,' he explained, rubbing his nose against hers.

'Oh, I see. You've come over all macho, have you?' She grinned at him, her hazel eyes full of amusement and something that he didn't dare put a name to because it was too soon and too scary to imagine that she might be falling in love with him. 'Just so long as you don't start dragging me back to camp by my hair then I suppose I can put up with it.'

'I can't make any promises,' he told her rather thickly because the word 'love' had clogged up his throat. Rachel didn't love him; she couldn't. Not yet...

'Did you come here specially to find me or did you just feel like a breather?' she asked, nestling into his arms.

'Both.' He cleared his throat, wished with all his heart that he could clear his head as well, but the thought had stuck like a limpet and was clinging on. Maybe Rachel didn't love him yet but she might love him in the future. Would that be a good or a bad thing?

'I'm glad you did because I wanted to talk to you.' She took hold of his hand, smiling as she studied the difference in their sizes. 'You have such beautiful hands,' she murmured.

'Thank you. I'd happily return the compliment but if I started listing all the beautiful things about you we'd be here all night.'

'Compliments from a caveman?' Her laughter was soft and sultry enough to make his pulse leap. 'Mind you don't spoil your image, macho-man!'

'I don't care. You *are* beautiful, Rachel, inside and out.' He kissed her gently on the mouth then drew back because he couldn't concentrate while he was doing that. 'So what did you want to talk to me about?'

'Tom.'

She took a deep breath that made her beautiful breasts rise beneath her T-shirt but he was far too stunned to appreciate the sight. It was all he could do not to leap up and run straight back to the camp because he really, *really* didn't want to hear anything else even though a short time ago he'd wanted to know all about the other guy. He sat frozen in agony as she continued.

'I need to sort out how I really feel about Tom and it would help if I could talk it over with you, Shiloh. Do you mind?'

Rachel had a horrible feeling that she might have made some sort of a social gaffe when Shiloh didn't reply. She bit her lip as the silence lengthened until it reached a point whereby she had to break it. 'I'm sorry…'

'If it would help…'

They both stopped and she saw him grimace. 'I was just going to say that if it will help then, yes, I'm happy to discuss your feelings about Tom.'

'You are?' Rachel frowned, not sure if she should believe him. After all, it was a lot to ask in view of what had happened last night…

Her mind veered away from that thought because she couldn't deal with it as well as everything else. Picking up a pebble, she tossed it into the river and watched the ripples spreading across the water. What she was doing could cause ripples, too—lots of them— and she was suddenly afraid because she didn't want to do anything that might damage her relationship with Shiloh.

'Yes. You need to be clear how you feel about Tom,' he said quietly and with such confidence that her fears were immediately allayed. 'Am I right to assume he's the same guy you mentioned last night, the one you were going on holiday with?'

'Mmm.' A little heat ran up her throat because it wasn't easy to mention last night in this present context. 'Tom and I went out together for almost a year. He was a registrar on the surgical team at Dalverston General and that's how we met.'

'I see. Did you live together?'

'No. We were planning on getting our own flat after we came back from holiday but the idea fell through along with all our other plans,' she explained, unable to keep the ache out of her voice because it still hurt to remember those days.

'So what happened? Was there someone else involved and is that why you split up?'

'No, nothing like that. It would have been easier in a way if it had been that simple.' She sighed. 'I told you about my sister's accident, didn't I? Well, what I didn't mention was that my niece was also injured in the crash. She was trapped inside the mini-bus and had to have the lower part of her leg amputated because there was no way to get her out otherwise. Tom was the surgeon who amputated it.'

'And it caused problems?' he said slowly, weighing up every word.

'Yes. Bethany was only fifteen at the time and she was heartbroken. Losing her leg as well as losing her mother was just too much for her to cope with. She ended up blaming Tom even though he'd had no choice. The situation became very fraught and in the end Tom accepted a post on the exchange scheme and moved to America to work. And that was that.'

'Only it wasn't that simple.' He sighed. 'Nothing ever is.'

'No. It took me ages to get over it but I had Beth to think about and that helped. Between working and looking after her I didn't have the time to think about myself. I just put my head down and kept going because there was nothing else I could do in the circumstances.'

'Did you never hope that Tom would come back one day?'

'At first I did but then I heard that he'd been offered a permanent post and had decided to stay in Miami.'

'You didn't write to each other?'

'No. Tom thought it would be best if we had a clean break. I just wanted to make life as easy as possible for all us so went along with it.'

'And now you've met up again here in Mexico and there are all sorts of unresolved issues between you?'

'I'm not sure I'd go so far as to say that,' she said slowly, because it didn't feel as though the situation was unresolved. Granted, she'd been surprised to see Tom again and confused because of the suddenness of it. But unresolved issues? No.

Her brain seemed to clear all of a sudden and she turned to Shiloh with a smile of relief, only he wasn't looking at her. He was staring into the water and there was an expression on his face that filled her with dread because it seemed as though he was already shutting her out.

'Look, Shiloh, I need to explain—' she began urgently, then broke off when there was a shout from the direction of the camp.

Shiloh stood up and looked back along the path. 'I wonder what's going on?'

'I don't know.' Rachel had just scrambled to her feet when Liam Danson came racing towards them. He was out of breath when he reached them and could hardly speak.

'There's been an accident in the town,' he gasped. 'Part of the church has fallen in and trapped about a dozen people inside. Brian Parker's one of them, apparently.'

'What in the name of blazes was he doing there?' Shiloh demanded, then shook his head. 'Forget it. It doesn't matter. We'll take a team straight into the town for speed. You, me, one of the Americans—'

'I'm coming, too,' Rachel put in quickly. 'I'm on duty tonight so it's only fair,' she added when it looked as though he might object.

'All right. You'll need sturdy shoes, a torch, gloves…'

'I know. I'll go and get ready.' She turned and ran back to the camp. June was in their tent and Rachel put her arm round her when she saw how upset the older woman looked.

'Try not to worry too much, June. Shiloh's taking a team into the town so he'll be there when they dig Brian out. He'll be fine, you'll see.'

'He'd better be or I'll give him hell!' June declared, sniffing. 'Are you going along as well?'

'Yes.'

Rachel found her boots then took a long-sleeved shirt out of her haversack and put it on over her T-shirt to stop the mosquitoes making a meal of her. June had a torch on a strap which she could wear round her head and she gave it to her.

'Thanks.' Rachel slipped it over her head and tightened the band then ran outside and found that Shiloh was already waiting, the truck engine ticking over and a mound of medical supplies loaded into the back. Tom was there as well but Rachel had more important things to worry about right then. Brian was a really nice guy and she couldn't bear to think of him being injured.

She hauled herself into the cab and slammed the door. Shiloh waited only long enough for the others to climb into the back before he set off. Rachel clung onto the door as the truck bounced over all the potholes until they reached the highway. They picked up speed then, the truck's headlamps lighting up the sky as they hurtled towards the town.

Rachel took a deep breath. She had no idea what she would have to deal with that night but she'd cope because Shiloh would be right there beside her. She'd never trusted anyone the way she trusted him and it was a mind-opening experience to realise it. Maybe she'd had doubts about her feelings for Tom but she was very sure how she felt about Shiloh. He was a man in a million and there was no one who could ever match up to him.

CHAPTER SEVEN

'*SILENCIO!*'

Shiloh paused when the man in charge of the rescue called for silence. They'd been working for well over an hour by that point, shifting the stones with their bare hands because it had been too dangerous to use a digger, and he was exhausted. It was only the thought of Brian being buried under all the rubble that was keeping him going.

'*Aqui!*'

A cheer rang out when one of the men pointed to a spot from where he'd heard voices issuing. Everyone set to with renewed vigour and ten minutes later the first survivor was pulled out. Shiloh quickly examined the woman but, apart from some cuts and bruises, she seemed to be fine. He handed her over to Rachel and went back to help with the digging, relieved that he'd been able to persuade Rachel to stay away from the site. She'd been keen to help with the rescue but he'd managed to convince her that they needed to set up a makeshift surgery in the back of the truck and had asked her to see to it. Maybe it was politically incorrect to want to keep her away from the danger but there was no way he was prepared to risk her getting hurt.

Half an hour later they'd brought everyone out. As luck would have it, the survivors had been close to the entrance when the church had collapsed so only part of the rubble had needed to be moved. Two people had sustained quite severe injuries so Liam and Tom had borrowed another truck and driven them back to camp while he and Rachel had stayed on to help. Brian was the last person to be brought out so Shiloh led him straight to their truck and made him sit on the tailboard while he examined him.

'You had a lucky escape,' he observed, checking the other man's skull for any sign of injuries. 'By rights you should be flat as the proverbial pancake after that little lot falling on top of you.'

'Ow!' Brian grimaced when Shiloh found a tender spot on the back of his head where a chunk of falling masonry must have hit him. He looked beseechingly at Rachel. 'Can't you do this, Rachel? I'm sure you'd treat me gently, unlike some I could mention.'

'Don't be a such a baby,' she scolded, grinning at him. She stepped forward and took hold of his hand. 'Here, I'll hold your hand for you if you think it will help.'

'Oh, it will, it will!' Brian returned, leering at her.

Shiloh ignored the exchange as he took a torch out of his pocket and shone it into Brian's eyes. It was funny because he didn't feel the least bit bothered when Brian held Rachel's hand yet he could have spat tacks when he'd seen Tom hugging her earlier that day. It just seemed to prove that the relationship she had with Tom was vastly different to what she had with anyone else. Even though he'd had no idea at the time what had gone on between them in the past, he had picked up on the vibes. His heart sank because it was yet more proof that Tom still meant a great deal to her.

'OK, you'll live. We'll keep you in the hospital tonight because of that knock on your head although I'm not anticipating any problems,' he told Brian tersely as he switched off the torch.

'Does that mean I get the full works—lots of lovely TLC?' Brian asked hopefully.

'It certainly does.' Rachel chuckled as she let go of his hand and started tidying up. 'June's on duty tonight and I'm sure she will lavish you with lots of attention after she's torn you off a strip!'

'Great! She's worse than my mother when she gets going, and that's saying something,' Brian groaned.

'She's only looking out for you,' Shiloh observed unsympathetically because he didn't have any sympathy to spare. 'What were you doing here in the first place? I thought you held your counselling sessions during the day?'

'Oh, um, yes, that's right,' Brian agreed sheepishly. 'I just wanted a word with one of the Australian search and rescue team. They're flying home in the morning and I wanted to catch her before she left.'

Shiloh let the subject drop because he could tell Brian was embarrassed. Was this another example of the course of true love not running smoothly? he wondered as he helped to clear everything away.

He sighed because a week ago the thought wouldn't even have occurred to him. He'd had his emotions so tightly buttoned up that love and the problems it caused wouldn't have been an issue. It just seemed to hammer home to him how dangerous it would be to let this situation with Rachel continue. He was on the brink of forgetting all his rules and he knew how painful it could turn out to be. How awful it would be if he allowed himself to fall in love with a woman who was in love with someone else.

The thought stayed with him for the rest of the night. Shiloh spent a miserable eight hours in his tent, going over and over what had happened and what he had to do. Even though he hated the idea, he knew that he had to cut himself off from Rachel while he was still capable of doing so. If she was still in love with Tom then it would be the best thing all round. He certainly didn't want to complicate matters by making her think that she had to take any account of his feelings. If there was a chance of her finding happiness again with Tom Hartley, he wouldn't get in the way.

Rachel was up early the next morning. She'd spent a restless night because she'd had so much on her mind. Although it had helped to clarify her thoughts by talking about Tom, she still felt very unsettled because she had no idea what Shiloh must be thinking. They'd been interrupted before she could tell him that she was almost sure she was over Tom and she needed to set the record straight. She went straight to the mess tent as soon as she was dressed, hoping that she might find him, but there was nobody there except Tom. Rachel stopped but there was no way that she could ignore Tom when he called her over.

'You're up bright and early this morning, Rachel. Couldn't you sleep either?'

'No. Must have been all the excitement,' she replied lightly, helping herself to a cup of coffee then sitting down.

'I know what you mean. Meeting up with you again was the last thing I expected, too, when I volunteered for this trip, but I'm not sorry it's happened,' Tom replied, completely unaware that she'd been referring to the excitement of rescuing Brian from the church. Rachel was just about to correct him when he forestalled her.

'I've always believed that things happen for a reason and this just proves it. It's too much of a coincidence that we should suddenly meet up again in the middle of nowhere, isn't it? It's as though it was pre-ordained.'

Rachel knew she had to say something before Tom got too carried away. 'It was a lovely surprise to see you again…'

'For me, too. I've missed you so much, sweetheart,' he murmured, placing his hands on her shoulders and pulling her towards him so he could kiss her.

It happened so fast and his kiss was just so familiar that Rachel instantly found herself transported back to those heady days when her love for Tom had filled her life with meaning. Tom had been the first man she'd fallen in love with and the first man she'd slept with as well. Maybe it was that memory that stopped her pushing him away.

'Wow!' He drew back and there was an expression in his eyes that made her blush. 'I'd forgotten how wonderful it was to kiss you.' He lifted her hand to his lips and tenderly kissed her palm. 'How did I ever find the strength to let you go?'

'I don't know,' she murmured because she felt so confused again that she could barely think. Tom's kiss had been nothing like Shiloh's but she'd enjoyed it. Did it mean that she still cared for Tom and was that why she'd kissed him back instead of pushing him away? Yet how could she care for Tom when she felt this way about Shiloh?

'I'm sorry to interrupt you, Rachel, but June wants to know if you could relieve her.'

The gravelly sound of Shiloh's voice made her

jump. She felt her stomach sink when she looked round and saw him standing in the entrance to the tent. Had he seen Tom kissing her just now? she wondered sickly. She had no idea but the thought that he might have witnessed what had happened filled her with apprehension.

'I know you're not on duty yet but June has a migraine. I'm sure she'd feel better if she could lie down,' he continued when she didn't reply.

'Yes, of course. Sorry.' Rachel shot to her feet and hurried to the exit but she had a horrible feeling that something awful was about to happen.

'I'll catch up with you later, Rachel,' Tom called after her, and she nodded because she couldn't think of anything to say. Shiloh stepped aside to let her pass and the way he took such care not to let their bodies touch was more than she could bear. She stopped and looked at him, unable to keep the hurt out of her eyes.

'Have I done something to upset you?'

'Of course not.' He turned and walked across the clearing but Rachel ran after him.

'Don't walk away! This is important.' She grabbed hold of his arm and made him stop, feeling her anger rising when he stared over the top of her head. 'You saw Tom kissing me just now, didn't you?'

'Yes.'

'Is that why you're upset?' she asked more gently.

'What you and Tom choose to do is your business.

It has absolutely nothing to do with me, Rachel,' he said flatly, so flatly, in fact, that her heart lurched. He was deliberately distancing himself from her and the idea terrified her.

'That's rubbish and you know it!' she declared, shaking his arm in a probably futile bid to get through to him. 'You can't just claim that you don't care after what happened between us the other night.'

'Of course I care!' He swung round to face her and his eyes blazed into hers, emerald flames lighting their depths and making her breath catch when she saw them.

'Shiloh, please...'

'Don't. There's no point talking about it.'

'The *point* is that we slept together. I don't know about you, but I'm certainly not in the habit of jumping into bed with someone at the drop of a hat!'

'And that's why I want everything to be right for you this time. It may sound trite but these things happen, Rachel, although I'm not going to insult you by dismissing it as a one-night stand. It meant a lot more than that to me, as it did to you.' His tone grated with emotion and her eyes filled with tears.

'It did. It was the most wonderful night...'

'No, please, don't say anything else.' He touched her gently on the mouth then let his hand fall to his side. 'What happened that night is something I shall never forget but it was just one night out of a whole lifetime and I don't want it to affect your future happiness.'

He shrugged but there was a mistiness about his eyes that told her how difficult he was finding it to hold back his own tears. 'I have nothing to offer you, Rachel, so it would be wrong for me to try and influence you in any way. If you and Tom can find happiness together again then I'm happy for you, too.'

'And that's it?' she asked numbly.

'Yes. That's it.'

He turned and walked away, only this time Rachel didn't stop him. She went to the hospital and relieved June even though what she wanted to do was to curl up into a ball and hide. There was a pain the size of Africa in her chest and a leadenness in her spirits that weighed her down but she had a job to do and she would do it well. Even though there was no room for her in Shiloh's life, she wouldn't let him down.

She got through the day somehow but she was functioning on autopilot for most of the time. Even though she respected Shiloh for being so honest, it didn't ease the pain of his rejection. It felt so much worse than when she'd split up with Tom that there had to be some deeper significance in that thought, only she was too upset to work it out. There was no point anyway because it wouldn't change anything. Shiloh didn't want her.

* * *

Two more days passed and Shiloh had to admit they were two of the most difficult days of his entire life. Rachel was walking around the camp like a ghost and he couldn't bear to see how she was suffering. He had to stop himself saying anything to her but he knew that he didn't have the right to interfere. If she needed help then the best person to provide it was Tom.

The last patients were finally transferred to the local hospital on the Friday morning then it was time to pack up. Shiloh contacted the airline that handled their travel arrangements but although there was no problem about flying their equipment back to England, there were no seats available from Mexico City for almost a week. The best the airline could offer him was a flight from Cancun in three days' time so he accepted that then contacted Natalie and got the response he'd expected. The whole team would spend three days in Cancun courtesy of her father, who had a villa there.

He hung up, wishing with all his heart that he could have just got on a plane and gone home. Oh, everyone would be delighted at the prospect of a few days R and R by the beach, everyone apart from him and Rachel, that was. The thought of having to prolong her agony was more than he could bear so he decided that he had to do something about it. If the American team agreed to join them at the villa then at least she would have Tom there and that would help to ease the situation for her.

They set off for Cancun first thing on Saturday morning. All their equipment had been crated up by then and sent by road to Mexico City. Mike Rafferty had offered to go with it and supervise the loading then make his own way home. Shiloh suspected that Mike was reluctant to accept Natalie's hospitality but he didn't say anything. Everyone needed to sort out their problems in their own way, as he'd done.

It was a bit of a squeeze fitting everyone in for the long drive to the coast. Shiloh was driving one of the trucks and David Preston was in charge of the other. June and Jolene piled into the cab with him, Katie and Alison went with David, and the rest divided themselves between the two trucks. As Shiloh started the engine he couldn't help checking to see if Rachel had opted to travel with his party but there was no sign of her or Tom. They must have decided to go with David. Together.

The thought hummed away at the back of his mind during the long drive east. He kept having mental flashes of her and Tom clinging together as they bounced over the ruts and had to grit his teeth to stop himself swearing. When Jolene and June begged for a comfort stop around noon, he gave in with ill grace because the sooner they reached Cancun the better. At least he wouldn't have to keep imagining Rachel clinging to Tom's manly arm!

They stopped at a tiny village on the edge of the jungle and caused quite a stir. People came rushing out of their houses to see what was happening. Shiloh dredged up enough Spanish to introduce himself to the local mayor and explain where they were going.

The mayor wanted to know all about them so Shiloh ended up sitting down in front of his house and telling him about the work they'd been doing while the rest of the group went off to attend to their needs. There were a lot of children running about and he smiled when he saw one little boy edging closer to them.

'Hola! Como estas, pequeño?'

The child smiled shyly and scuttled closer, crouching down a few feet away from where Shiloh was sitting. Like all the local children he was extremely thin but his skin had an unhealthy grey tinge to it and his black eyes appeared sunk in his head. Shiloh frowned because there was something about the child's appearance that had triggered an alarm bell.

'Has he been ill?' he asked the mayor, and listened intently as the man explained that little Miguel had hurt his head a few weeks earlier and that ever since then he'd been drinking and passing vast amounts of water. Apparently, the boy's mother desperately wanted him to see a doctor but it was too far to take him to the nearest town. She was a widow with four other children to take care of and didn't have the money for the bus fares.

'I'll take a look at him,' Shiloh offered, standing up. 'Can you find his mother?'

The mayor hurried away and came back a few minutes later with a woman who looked far too young to be the mother of five children. Shiloh explained that he was a doctor and that he would examine the child if she wanted him to.

'*Si, si! Muchas gracias,*' she agreed eagerly.

Shiloh hunkered down in front of the boy and studied him carefully, taking note of the dry, cracked lips. The child gave every appearance of being dehydrated despite drinking an excessive amount of water. Taking hold of the boy's hand, he gently pinched a small flap of skin and could tell at once that it had lost its normal elasticity which was another sure sign that the boy was dehydrated.

'Problems?'

Shiloh glanced up when he heard Rachel's voice, praying that she couldn't tell how wonderful it was to hear her speaking to him. She'd made a point of avoiding him for the past few days and he'd missed the sweet sound of her voice more than he cared to admit. He cleared his throat, wanting to be sure that he didn't give himself away.

'Looks like it. Apparently, he injured his head a few weeks ago and hasn't been himself ever since. He's been drinking excessively and passing large amounts of urine. He looks to me as though he's extremely dehydrated as well.'

'D'you think he's diabetic?'

'That's what I was wondering although it would rule out any connection with the head injury. Maybe it's just a coincidence that he started being ill straight afterwards. Still, it's easy enough to check. Would you mind fetching my case out of the truck? There should be a glucose testing kit in it.'

'Will do.'

She hurried away and Shiloh carried on with his examination—checking the boy's head and neck then his eyes. Rachel came back with his bag and, without needing to be asked, got out the glucose kit and passed it to him.

'Thanks.' Shiloh took it from her, fumbling slightly when their hands touched. A haze suddenly clouded his vision and he had to breathe deeply before he could continue. It alarmed him that just the touch of her hand should have had such a marked effect that it was an effort to concentrate on what he was doing.

'I just need to prick his finger to get a drop of blood,' he explained to the child's mother, showing her the tiny needle. 'It won't hurt him.'

She nodded slowly, obviously unsure about what was happening, and Shiloh smiled at her. 'He'll be fine. Don't worry.'

'Let me clean his hand before you do that.' Rachel grabbed an antiseptic wipe from the pack and knelt beside him.

Shiloh's heart started bucking like the wildest
bronco when her shoulder came to rest against his.
He tried a bit more deep breathing—in and out with
several repeats—but it didn't help. Blood pumped
from his heart, sending a tidal wave of heat around
his body so that he had to physically restrain himself
from jumping to his feet. It was pure torture to have
her crouched there beside him and not be able to
touch her.

'That's better,' she announced, glancing round,
and he somehow managed to gain enough control
over himself to continue—pricking the boy's finger
and quickly smearing the drop of blood it produced
onto the chemically coated strip in the monitor. He
frowned when he saw the reading because his initial
diagnosis, that the boy was diabetic, obviously
wasn't correct.

'His glucose levels are fine,' Rachel observed in
surprise, peering over his shoulder.

'So it appears. Bang goes that theory,' he said flip-
pantly because he couldn't have managed serious
right then even if he'd tried. *Serious* encompassed all
sorts of things and not just the child's condition.
Under the heading of *serious* there was a list of items
ranging from how his body responded whenever he
and Rachel touched right the way up to the fact that
he was falling in love with her. That would have to
be at the very top of the list, of course, because it
was the most serious thing that could have happened

to him. He was falling in love with Rachel so what should he do about it? Should he tell her? Or should he keep it to himself?

It was his decision but as he crouched there in the dust, Shiloh knew that it wasn't only his life which would be affected by it. If he told Rachel then it would have huge repercussions for her, too. She'd only just met Tom again and hadn't had enough time to decide how she felt about him. If he himself told her that he thought he was falling in love with her, she'd find it even more difficult to make up her mind. Was he really prepared to take the risk of her making a mistake?

Shiloh knew the answer to that question without having to think about it. He'd been through enough heartache when Sally had died and he refused to put himself through any more. It would be better to spend the rest of his life alone than live with the constant fear that one day Rachel might leave him.

CHAPTER EIGHT

RACHEL wasn't sure what was happening but there was definitely something going on because she could feel the back of her neck prickling. She was just about to ask Shiloh what was wrong when Tom appeared.

'What's up?' Tom asked, squatting down beside them.

'Shiloh was just checking to see if the boy is diabetic,' she explained, unable to decide if she was glad of the interruption or resented it. She glanced at Shiloh but he appeared completely focused on the child and she frowned. Had she imagined that something had been worrying him just now?

'The reading looks fine to me so why did you think he was diabetic?' Tom asked curiously.

'Because he's been suffering from excessive thirst and polyuria,' Shiloh replied curtly, so curtly, in fact, that Rachel blinked. It was unlike Shiloh to be so brusque with members of the team and she couldn't understand why he'd singled Tom out for such treatment now—unless he was jealous of Tom's attention to her.

'And that's it?' Tom countered in the same forth-

123

right manner. 'It could be anything from psychogenic polydipsia to kidney failure from those symptoms.'

'So it could.' Shiloh stood up. 'It could also be diabetes insipidus and I'm leaning more towards that diagnosis now.'

'Sounds more like a shot in the dark to me,' Tom sneered. 'You know as well as I do how rare diabetes insipidus is so what makes you imagine it could be that?'

Rachel listened while the two men held an increasingly chilly discussion about the pros and cons of the theory. Naturally, Shiloh was very much in favour of it and listed all the salient facts to back it up. Tom, however, seemed equally determined not to accept it. They batted the idea back and forth until her head was reeling from listening to them. Something needed to be done to bring the discussion to an amicable conclusion so it was a relief when June appeared and demanded to know what was going on.

'Shiloh and Tom were just discussing this little boy's condition,' Rachel explained, determined to remain neutral although she couldn't believe how pigheaded they were both being.

'Ah, so it's a discussion, is it?' June looked from one to the other. 'I thought you two were arguing but it just goes to show how wrong a person can be.'

Rachel hid her smile when she saw a rim of colour run along Shiloh's cheekbones. He didn't reply as he crouched down and spoke to Miguel's mother. June rolled her eyes as she drew Rachel to one side.

'They're acting like a couple of kids in the school playground. What set them off, or is that a daft question?'

'What d'you mean?' Rachel asked, puzzled.

'Oh, come on, love, it's obvious what was going on!' June sighed when she still looked blank. 'They were trying to outdo each other for your benefit. To put it bluntly—they were showing off.'

'Oh, no, of course they weren't,' she protested, but June just smiled.

'Oh, yes, they were and it really worries me. If Shiloh is prepared to go head to head like that with Tom then it means only one thing. He cares about you, Rachel, so I hope you'll take that into account.'

'I care about him, too,' she admitted. 'But you're wrong, June, because he doesn't care about me the way you mean. He's already made it clear that we don't have a future so there's no need to worry about him.'

'Has he indeed? Well, from what I've just seen, maybe he needs to remember that himself. For a man who isn't interested he's giving out some very strange signals, that's all I can say.'

June left it at that and went to join the others. Rachel bit her lip as she watched her walking away. Was June right? Did Shiloh wish that he hadn't pushed her away? There was no way of telling unless she asked him and she couldn't face the thought of doing that and maybe suffering another rejection.

'Is Smith always so bloody-minded? He seems to believe that he's always right and everyone else is always wrong!'

Rachel glanced round when a disgruntled Tom came over to her. 'Actually, I've always found him to be very open-minded whenever I've made a suggestion.'

'Why doesn't that surprise me?' Tom replied dryly. 'It's obvious the guy fancies you, Rachel. That's why he came on so strong with me just now. He resents the fact that you and I have something going for us.'

Rachel couldn't decide what to say first, whether she should deny that Shiloh fancied her or tell Tom off for assuming there was still something between them. She still hadn't made up her mind when Shiloh approached them.

'I'm leaning more and more towards the idea that it's diabetes insipidus,' he announced, completely ignoring Tom as he addressed her. 'According to the boy's mother, he suffered quite a severe head injury a few weeks ago when he fell off some rocks.'

'And that could have caused diabetes insipidus?' she queried, hoping to defuse the situation by focusing on work. It obviously hadn't worked, she decided, when Tom walked away.

'Yes, it's possible. Diabetes insipidus is something

entirely separate from diabetes mellitus. It isn't an inability to absorb glucose that causes the disorder and has nothing to do with the production of insulin by the pancreas,' Shiloh explained, obviously unfazed by the other man's abrupt departure.

'I've heard about it although I'm rather hazy about the details,' she admitted, determined not to be sidetracked. It was up to Tom and Shiloh to sort out their differences.

'It's quite rare so that's one thing Hartley and I agree on at least. Diabetes insipidus usually results from the failure of the pituitary gland to secrete enough vasopressin—that's the hormone that regulates the amount of water passed by the kidneys. Sometimes the problem arises as a result of a tumour forming around the pituitary gland but in those cases there's usually other symptoms as well—visual disturbance, headaches and so on. In other instances the pituitary gland has been damaged in some way, either through head trauma or disease. I think Miguel falls into that category.'

'I see. You think he damaged the pituitary gland when he fell off the rocks. It makes sense but what's the solution?' Rachel frowned as she looked at the little boy. 'Can he be treated with drugs? I'm sure I read something once about a nasal spray being used to treat patients with this condition.'

'That's right. Desmopressin in a spray form is used to treat it but the problem is that drugs are very expensive.' He grimaced. 'I doubt if the family has enough money to pay for the medication he needs.'

'But surely there's something we can do to help,' Rachel protested.

'Obviously, we need to organise some tests first to make sure it is diabetes insipidus we're dealing with. I'll arrange for a urine sample to be tested at the local clinic and give Miguel's mother the money for the bus fares as well as a letter for the doctor.

'As for any drugs he might need, I'll try to arrange funding to pay for them. Natalie's family has set up a charitable trust to help people in circumstances such as these so I'll contact the trustees as soon as we get to Cancun.' He sighed. 'Making sure Miguel takes the medication on a regular basis could be our biggest problem, though.'

'But you'll find a way round it?' she pleaded, hating to think of the child's condition growing worse.

'I'll do my best.' He laughed. 'I'll have to because I don't think I could bear to let you down as well as that poor kid!'

'Thank you,' she said softly, knowing that her expression said far more than the actual words had done. Her heart ached when he visibly withdrew into himself. It hurt to know that Shiloh was determined to maintain this distance between them. She longed to tell him there was no need but how could she when she still had to decide how she really felt about Tom?

In the end, she did nothing and went back to the truck, leaving Shiloh to explain to the boy's mother what he wanted her to do. However, the thought of spending more time with him while she felt this way wasn't easy. She'd always been a person who'd known her own mind in the past so it was doubly difficult to deal with these uncertainties. On the one hand she knew that Shiloh meant a great deal to her but she couldn't just dismiss the fact that Tom's kiss had reminded her of how it had been between them. Yet in her heart she knew that if Shiloh weren't being so reticent then the situation would be so much clearer. But if he didn't want her...

The villa was like something out of a film set and Rachel wasn't the only one who gasped in amazement when they drew up in the courtyard a few hours later. She climbed out of the truck, ignoring her aching muscles as she looked around.

'It's fantastic!' Katie declared. 'Just look at all those flowers and that fountain and...and *everything*!'

'If I'm dreaming then, *please*, don't wake me up,' Daniel pleaded as he came to join them. He sighed as he stared at the huge, pink-painted villa. 'Talk about how the other half lives, eh?'

'It's gorgeous,' Rachel agreed. 'Just look at that view. We're right on the beach. We'll be able to roll out of bed and into the sea!'

'Now, that *does* sound tempting.' Tom said. 'Can't you just imagine us getting up each morning and running down to cool off in that surf?'

'Um, yes,' Rachel murmured. She bit her lip when she saw the knowing look Daniel and Katie exchanged. It was obvious they had picked up on the implication of Tom's words, and she knew that she had to make it clear to Tom that they wouldn't be sharing a room. She waited until the other couple went off to explore the gardens before she rounded on him.

'Look, Tom, I don't know what you imagine is going to happen but you and I are *not* going to be sharing a bedroom while we're here.'

'I'm sorry. I got a bit carried away.' He sighed. 'I suppose it was thinking about that holiday we had planned that did it, but I never meant to embarrass you. D'you want me to have a word with the others and explain?'

'No, there's no need to do that,' she said quickly, not wanting to make an issue out of it. She smiled, thinking how typical it was that he'd let his enthusiasm get the better of him. Tom had always had an impulsive streak—it had been one of the things that had attracted her to him in the first place, in fact. She'd always been the sort of person who thought first and acted second so Tom's spontaneity had been an appealing contrast. Mind you, she seemed to have changed recently. She hadn't stopped to think before she'd made love with Shiloh, had she?

The thought made her blush and she turned away before Tom could ask her what was wrong. Picking up her haversack, she made her way into the villa and followed the sound of voices until she came to the bedrooms. The house was all on one level so each of the bedrooms had sliding glass doors leading onto the gardens. Rachel stopped outside the room June and Alison had commandeered for themselves.

'Think you'll be comfortable enough in here?' she teased, taking stock of the gleaming marble flooring, the honey-coloured walls and matching silk drapes.

'It will be tough but we'll manage,' June declared, her tongue very firmly in her cheek.

Rachel laughed and left them to unpack. She carried on along the corridor until she came to a room that nobody seemed to have chosen. This room was decorated in shades of coffee and cream and once again there was a marble floor and silk drapes at the windows. It was a little haven of luxury after the rigours of the past two weeks and she soaked it all up.

'Oops, sorry! My mistake. I thought this room was free.'

She glanced round when Shiloh came barging in and grinned at him. 'You're too late, I've bagged it for myself!'

'Typical! You women don't waste any time getting the best of the deal,' he accused, returning her smile with one that made her knees suddenly knock. He seemed to have forgotten that he was supposed to be acting distant and elusive and there was no denying that the warmth in his eyes was having an effect.

'You wouldn't begrudge a poor hard-working nurse a couple of days of luxury?' she responded in her most pitiful tone because she didn't want to scare him off by letting him see how she felt.

'What was that?' He cupped a hand to his ear and pretended to listen. 'I could have sworn I heard the sound of violins just then.'

'You horrible man!' She picked up one of the coffee-coloured cushions from the chaise longue and threatened him with it.

'Pax!' he pleaded, cowering into the corner.

'Humph! It's a good job I'm such a wonderfully kind person otherwise you'd pay for that snide remark, Smith!' she told him, pretending to glower as she put the cushion back in its rightful place.

'I know, and I really, *really* appreciate your kindness, Sister Hart.' His smile was so wicked and sexy that Rachel's heart stumbled. She'd missed their playful exchanges in the last few days so much. Something of what she was feeling must have shown on her face because he abruptly sobered.

'I never meant to make life difficult for you, Rachel.'

'I know.' She managed a smile but her mouth kept trying to turn down at the corners instead of up and he sighed.

'You are just too kind, that's the trouble. Another woman would have told me to go to hell and that would have been the end of the matter.'

'I can't do that, Shiloh, because I don't want you to go to hell or anywhere else.'

'No?' His voice rumbled up from his chest and her hands clenched when she realised the struggle he was having to keep control of his emotions. Had June been right? Did he regret his decision to cut her out of his life and would he be prepared to reconsider? Maybe she still had a few concerns about her feelings for Tom but she had no doubts as to how she felt about Shiloh. He meant so much to her, far too much to let him go out of her life for good.

'No. I want to—'

'So here you are! I've been looking *everywhere* for you.'

All of a sudden Tom was there. Rachel saw Shiloh stiffen when he spotted the suitcase in Tom's hand. She knew immediately that he thought she'd arranged to share the room with Tom and the need to set him straight was so great that her vocal cords knotted themselves into clumps in panic. She could only watch helplessly in silence as Shiloh curtly excused himself and left.

'Sorry. Did I come at a bad time?' Tom asked with a frown.

'It doesn't matter,' she replied, finding it bitterly ironic that she had no difficulty speaking now. Picking up her bag, she placed it on the bed and unzipped the top, trying not to think about the expression on Shiloh's face as he'd left. If he'd been determined to set some distance between them before then it was nothing to what he was planning on doing now.

'I just came to see if you fancy a swim after you finish unpacking,' Tom explained. 'Everyone's decided to go to the beach and I said I'd ask you.'

'Sounds good,' she agreed because it was the fastest way she could think of to get rid of him.

'Great stuff! I'm just down the corridor—third door on the left—so give me knock when you're ready,' he told her, smiling broadly as he backed out of the room.

Rachel carried on unpacking after he'd left. Most of her clothes were in dire need of a wash so she just found her swimsuit and dropped the rest on the floor then went into the bathroom and took a shower. The water was hot and plentiful and she let it pour over her, hoping it would wash away the pain as well as the dust. It was only when she realised that some of the moisture on her cheeks came from her own tears that she admitted the futility of that hope. Nothing could ease the heartache she'd felt at seeing Shiloh withdraw from her like that. Maybe he did care for her but his feelings weren't strong enough to overcome the trauma of what had happened to him in the past. She really couldn't blame him. If he didn't love her then why would he want to put himself at risk again?

She turned off the water and stood there while the thought sank in. It wasn't easy to face the truth but there was no way that she wanted to make the situation any more stressful for either of them. Shiloh didn't love her and never would. She had to accept that and get on with her life. Tom seemed keen for them to try again but how did she feel about the idea? Could she really imagine them renewing their former relationship? She sighed because she simply couldn't picture it happening, yet she knew exactly what she'd do if Shiloh told her that he wanted her. She would go to him immediately but she couldn't spend the rest of her life hoping Shiloh would change his mind.

Shiloh let himself into the guest house and tossed his bag onto the sofa. Crossing the room, he unlocked the window and pushed it wide open. He couldn't seem to breathe properly so he stood there for some time, drinking in huge lungfuls of air until he could function again.

He turned and stared around the luxurious apartment, wondering if it was possible to feel any more

wretched than he did at that moment. Knowing that
Rachel was planning on spending the next few nights
with Tom Hartley was almost more than he could
bear but there was nothing he could do about it. He'd
already told her they didn't have a future so how
could he now tell her that he'd changed his mind?
That his feelings for her had finally made him realise
that perhaps it was time to move on.

She'd think he was just saying that because he was
jealous of Tom and so he was—very jealous!—but
it wasn't right to keep turning her life inside out by
saying one thing then contradicting himself. He had
to stick to his decision and make sure she knew that
he'd meant it, too. It wasn't fair to Rachel to keep
vacillating so he would let her know that he was
happy for her and Tom even if it killed him, which
it might very well do! So long as Rachel was happy,
he would cope with his own heartache. He'd done it
before and he could do it again.

Dinner that night was to be a barbecue cooked for
them by the Mexican couple who looked after the
villa. All the women had decided to make a special
effort so the washer and dryer were in constant use
after they returned from the beach. Rachel finally got
her turn at the ironing board and pressed her newly
washed jeans as well as the blouse that Maria-Luz's
mother had given to her as a present.

She took the clothes back to her room and got

ready, wishing that she'd brought more than a tub of moisturiser and a lipstick with her on the trip. It would have been a welcome boost to know that she was looking her best.

She hadn't seen Shiloh since she'd come back from the beach because he'd gone into town to sort out the arrangements for Miguel. Even though she'd decided what she had to do, Rachel couldn't deny that she felt nervous as she made her way to the terrace where everyone had gathered. It was one thing to take a rational view of the situation when she and Shiloh were apart but it would be far more difficult to stick to it when they were together. All she could do was to stay in the background until everything had calmed down.

'Oh, wow! You look lovely, Rachel. That top is just *gorgeous* on you!'

Rachel groaned when Katie unwittingly drew everyone's attention to her as she stepped onto the terrace. She summoned a smile but she could have done without any fuss. Shiloh was standing on the edge of the group and she was very conscious of him looking at her as she went to join them.

'Thank you kindly. There's nothing like some good old-fashioned soap and water to bring out the best in a girl!'

'Oh, I don't know. A bit of dirt can be very attractive on the right person,' Brian mused.

Alison grinned. 'Especially if that person just happens to have an Aussie accent!'

Everyone laughed at the quip and Rachel breathed a sigh of relief when the conversation moved on. When Tom came over to ask her what she wanted to drink, she was able to respond quite naturally. 'A glass of wine would be nice.'

'Red or white?'

'Oh, red, I think.'

'Coming right up!'

He went off to fetch it and Rachel sat down on one of the cushioned loungers, thinking what a treat it was to be waited on. She spent so much of her time looking after other people that it was nice to be on the receiving end for a change.

'I spoke to the trustees about young Miguel. They've agreed to consider him for funding.'

Rachel felt her heart jolt nervously when Shiloh sat down beside her. 'That sounds promising,' she murmured, hoping she sounded suitably composed. 'When will you know for definite?'

'Next week. We still need to be sure what's wrong with him, of course.'

'Of course.'

'Once we have confirmation I'll make arrangements with the local clinic to stock the medication Miguel needs,' he continued. 'It shouldn't be a problem, though, because I spoke to the doctor in charge and he seemed perfectly happy to help, especially when I mentioned that the clinic might be in line for a grant from the trust.'

'I'm sure they'd be glad of some extra money,' she agreed, wondering where this was leading. Did Shiloh simply want to bring her up to date about Miguel or was there another reason for this conversation?

'They would. Their funds are pretty limited from what I could gather so any extra revenue will come in handy.' He glanced up when Tom came back with the drinks. Rachel saw an expression of indecision cross his face before he stood up. 'Anyway, that's enough about work. We're here to enjoy ourselves, not talk shop. Have a good evening, you two. You've earned it.'

'My, my, do my ears deceive me or was the great Shiloh Smith actually offering an olive branch?' Tom asked sarcastically, handing her a glass.

'Sounds like it.'

Rachel took a sip of the wine then put the glass down when she realised her hands were trembling. Tom said something to her and she responded, even laughed when June came over to tell them some long involved tale about her underwear falling to pieces in the washing machine. It was as though she was suddenly able to function on two separate levels. She could carry on a normal conversation while at the same time her heart was breaking.

She excused herself and walked to the edge of the

terrace. She could see the vast black swell of the ocean from there and she stared at it while she struggled to deal with what had just happened. Tom believed that Shiloh had been trying to make amends for his earlier brusqueness but she knew better. He had been giving her and Tom his blessing and she couldn't begin to describe how that made her feel because it was the last thing she wanted from him!

Tears stung her eyes but she blinked them away. She wouldn't cry, not here in front of everyone. She wouldn't make a show of herself or let Shiloh see how much it had hurt to have him dismiss what had happened between them. Maybe he believed that he'd done the right thing and maybe she would come to believe it, too, but at the moment it was impossible to imagine a time when his rejection wouldn't hurt. He had deliberately tried to push her into another man's arms and if that didn't prove he didn't love her then nothing would.

CHAPTER NINE

THE barbecue was followed by a display of Mexican dancing organised for them by the housekeeper, Consuelo, and her husband, Ramòn. Apparently, the couple supplemented their income by performing as part of a troupe that visited the local hotels and danced for the tourists. Rachel smiled and clapped along with everyone else as she watched the performance but her heart really wasn't in it. When Consuelo asked for volunteers she hung back, shaking her head when the woman urged her to join in.

'No, really. I'd rather not,' she protested, but the other nurses wouldn't hear of her sitting on the sidelines so in the end she was forced to give in.

Consuelo demonstrated the steps then gave them each one of the narrow shawls which all the Mexican women were wearing. She showed them how to loop it over their shoulders and tie it at their wrists. Rachel tried to appear as though she was having fun, no easy feat when her heart was almost numb with pain. Ramòn started up the music and she followed the other women, trying her best to keep in time with the pulsing beat. When the dancers from the troupe suddenly turned and looped their shawls around the necks of several of the men in the audience there was great hilarity. Not to be outdone, the other nurses each grabbed a partner until there was only her and Shiloh left.

'Come on, Rachel,' June urged. 'You can't let him get away!'

Rachel's heart was racing as she stepped forward and looped her shawl around Shiloh's neck. 'Sorry,' she murmured in a voice only he could hear.

'It's OK.' He rose to his feet and smiled tightly at her. 'I'd hate to be a killjoy.'

He placed his hands on her waist and Rachel almost leapt right out of her skin. It was only the fact that everyone was watching that stopped her pulling away. They circled the floor, her hands resting on Shiloh's chest, his hands gripping her waist; it felt so good, so right and yet every step was pure torture. It was a relief when the music stopped and everyone returned to their seats, laughing and teasing each other about who was the best dancer.

Rachel decided that she couldn't take any more. She summoned a smile when Tom came over to her. 'I'm worn out so I think I'll call it a night.'

'Me, too. I must be getting old because I can't seem to keep up these days,' he agreed cheerfully. He looped a friendly arm around her waist as he turned to the others. 'We're off to bed now. See you in the morning, folks!'

Rachel flushed when her discreet departure was suddenly turned into a major event. She saw Shiloh watching them and turned away because there was no point worrying about what he thought. He'd made it clear he didn't want her. She could do exactly what she liked and the thought was like a red-hot knife being stabbed through her heart.

'What's wrong, Rachel?' Tom stopped outside her bedroom and looked at her in concern. 'I can tell you're upset but I don't know why.'

'I'm fine,' she began, but he cut short her protests.

'No, you're not. You've been really edgy all night long and I want to know what's wrong. Is it my fault? Because if it is then I'd prefer it if you told me the truth.'

'It isn't you, Tom…well, not really. It's just such a mess!' Tears suddenly began to pour down her face and he sighed.

'I knew there was something worrying you. I could sense it.' He glanced round when he heard footsteps coming along the corridor. 'Sounds as though the others have decided to call it a night as well so shall we go into your room? It's a bit too public out here in the corridor to hold a conversation.'

'Yes, if you like.' Rachel led the way and sat down on the bed, wondering numbly what she was going to do. It hurt so much to know that Shiloh didn't want anything more to do with her. She looked up when Tom sat down beside her and took hold of her hand.

'I'd like to think we're still friends, Rachel, even if we can't be anything else. OK, I admit that I would love it if we could try again but if it isn't what you want then I'll have to accept that.'

'Oh, Tom, if only it was that easy!'

'If you still have any feelings for me then it is that easy.' He turned her to face him and looked deep into her eyes. 'You loved me once, Rachel, I know you did. Are you sure you still don't feel something for me?'

'I don't know how I feel at the moment,' she admitted brokenly because it was true.

'Then maybe this will help,' Tom murmured, bending so he could kiss her, yet the instant Rachel felt his mouth touch hers, she knew it wasn't what she wanted.

'No!' She pushed him away and jumped to her feet as everything came clearly into focus. She didn't want Tom or any other man because she wanted Shiloh! It was Shiloh she loved, and only Shiloh she wanted to kiss her. It wasn't fair to let Tom think there was a chance of them getting back together.

'I guess that answers my question.' Tom stood up and she was racked with guilt when she saw the hurt on his face.

'I'm so sorry, Tom.'

'It isn't your fault.' He summoned a smile and

Rachel felt even worse because he was being so kind. She put her arms around him and hugged him.

'I loved you such a lot, Tom. Really I did.'

'I know. I loved you, too, Rachel, just as much, but maybe I was wrong to think we could recapture the old magic. A lot of water has flown under the bridge since then, for me as well as for you.'

'What do you mean?'

'I met someone else after I moved to America. We were together for some time but in the end it didn't work out. We split up last month and that's why I volunteered for this trip.' He sighed. 'I needed to get away and rethink my life so I could decide what I wanted to do in the future.'

'And instead you met me and thought it would solve your problems if we got back together,' she suggested slowly.

'Something like that.' He laughed wryly. '*Exactly* like that, in fact. Will you forgive me?'

'There's nothing to forgive,' she assured him truthfully.

'Good.' He kissed her on the cheek. 'Thanks, Rachel, not just for being so understanding but for all the good times we had in the past. You were a very important part of my life and I have so many wonderful memories of our time together.'

'Me, too.'

She sat down on the bed after Tom left, thinking how strange it was that fate had brought them back

together at this point in time. Tom's life was in a
state of flux, too, and it was understandable that he
should have been confused about his feelings. In a
way she was glad it had happened because it had
helped clarify her own feelings. Although she would
always be fond of Tom, she wasn't in love with him.
How could she be when she was in love with Shiloh?

They arrived back at Heathrow in the early hours of
Tuesday morning. Shiloh had managed to find himself a seat on the plane well away from the rest of
the party and had spent the flight pretending to be
asleep. The last three days at the villa had been an
absolute nightmare. Even though he'd spent most of
his time in the guest house he hadn't been able to
cut himself off completely from what had been happening. Watching Rachel and Tom together had been
sheer purgatory. They'd looked so happy and so relaxed with each other that it had made him see how
foolish he'd been to imagine Rachel had ever cared
about him. The American team had flown home from
Cancun before them but even that hadn't helped because then he'd had to endure the sight of Rachel
moping about on her own. Frankly, he couldn't wait
to bring this whole miserable episode to its rightful
conclusion.

A bleary-eyed June came staggering over to say
goodbye. 'I'm getting too old for this malarkey.

Remind me to tell you to get lost the next time you invite me along on one of your jaunts!'

'You know you loved every minute of it,' Shiloh told her, making an effort to appear upbeat. Rachel had followed him through customs and was now saying goodbye to the others. Would she speak to him? he wondered. Or would she leave without saying anything to him?

The thought of her leaving like that was more than he could bear. Even though he knew he was just adding to his problems, he had to speak to her one last time. He kissed June then shook hands with Steven and Liam, refusing their offer to share a taxi with the excuse that he needed to check on their equipment before he left the airport. It was a pack of lies because Rafferty had already been in touch to let him know the cargo had arrived safely in England.

He waited until everyone had finished hugging each other then tapped Rachel on the arm. 'I just wanted to thank you for everything you've done. Your input was absolutely vital to the overall success of the mission, Rachel, and I really appreciate it.'

'I only did my job,' she replied lightly, and held out her hand. 'Thank you for taking me along on the trip, Shiloh. I gained a great deal from it.'

'I'm glad.' He summoned a smile, wishing he could stop himself asking the next question but knowing that he needed to hear the answer. 'I take it that you and Tom will be keeping in touch?'

'Oh, yes. There's no doubt about that,' she assured him as Katie came running over to tell her they were next in the taxi queue.

Shiloh stepped aside as the two women hurried away and the last sight he had of Rachel was of her back view. He took a deep breath, wondering hollowly how he was going to put his life back together after what had happened. He'd done it once before but something told him that this time it would be even more difficult. This time he would have to deal with the thought that Rachel was with Tom and he couldn't begin to describe how that made him feel. All he could do was hope that he'd get through it but it wasn't going to be easy. Letting Rachel go had been the hardest thing he'd ever done.

Rachel went back to work the following day. The children's ward at Dalverston General Hospital had always been one of the busiest departments and nothing had changed while she'd been away. The days flew past as she slotted back into the familiar routine. When a couple of members of staff went off sick with flu, she ended up working extra shifts to cover for them, but she didn't mind. At least while she was working she could forget what had happened in Mexico and that was something to be grateful for.

It was when she returned home after work that it was the most difficult to cope. She would spend her evenings going over and over everything that had happened between her and Shiloh. There wasn't even any respite when she went to bed because then she dreamt about him and awoke with tears streaming down her face. All she could do was hope that the situation would grow easier with time.

June passed then July and August arrived bringing an influx of tourists into the town. Dalverston was surrounded by some magnificent countryside and a lot of people used it as a base while they went exploring. The number of patients they treated at the hospital increased dramatically and the staff were stretched to their limits as they tried to keep up. Rachel ended up working twelve-hour shifts for a solid week and felt completely exhausted at the end of it. She went into town on her day off and bought a supply of vitamin pills in the hope they would give her the boost she needed but it was still an effort to drag herself out of bed the next morning.

She went into work, hoping they would have an easy day for once but, typically, it was non-stop from the time she took over from the night staff. They had three new admissions in the space of an hour. One was a five-year-old girl called Chloë Johnson who'd been admitted with suspected concussion after falling off a swing in the local playground.

Rachel got the child settled and was just about to write up her chart when Chloë was violently sick. There was just Rachel and a very new junior nurse on duty that morning so she stripped the bed herself rather than ask Caroline to do it then went to fetch a bowl of water to wash Chloë, sighing when she discovered there were no towels left on the shelf. They'd had agency nurses running the ward during the night and they hadn't replenished the supplies which meant she would have to do it.

Rachel went to the linen cupboard and switched on the light. The towels were kept on the top two shelves so she pulled over a stool and climbed up to get them then had to grab hold of the shelf when the room suddenly started to spin. She stepped off the stool and sat down until the dizziness had passed. Caroline poked her head round the cupboard door and looked at her in alarm.

'Are you OK, Rachel? You've gone a really funny colour.'

'I just felt a bit giddy.' She managed to smile when she saw how anxious the junior looked. 'I'll be fine in a moment so don't worry that I'm about to leave you in the lurch. What did you want me for?'

'Oh, yes, there's someone on the phone for you. I didn't catch her name, I'm afraid.'

Rachel bit back a sigh. Although Caroline was very willing, she was hopeless at taking messages. 'What did I tell you the other day about asking the caller to repeat their name? It's really important so try to remember it in the future, will you?'

'I did ask her to repeat it but it was a terrible line,'

Caroline replied indignantly. 'I couldn't hear what she said the second time either!'

'I see.' Rachel didn't feel well enough to point out that she should have kept on asking until she had the information she needed. She just stood up and pointed to the towels. 'Can you fetch some towels through, please? Chloë Johnson—the new admission in bed five—has been sick so she'll need sponging down and her bed will have to be remade.'

She left Caroline to deal with it and went to the office to sort out the phone call. It was a member of the admin staff, complaining that they hadn't received her quarterly report. Rachel didn't bother explaining that she'd not had time to do it. She just promised to get it done as soon as she could then went to see how Caroline was faring. The junior had finished mopping up little Chloë so Rachel helped her make the bed then had a word with the child's parents and explained that it wasn't unusual for someone suffering from concussion to be sick.

They seemed much happier after that so she left them to sit with their daughter and went back to the office, hoping to make a start on the report while it was quiet for once. She'd done the first month's statistics before she'd set off for Mexico so she just needed to dig out the figures for the last two months...

She stopped dead, her heart pounding as the full impact of that thought sank in. It was over two

months since she'd come back from Mexico and during that time she hadn't had her normal monthly pe-
riod. She'd always been extremely regular before so
was it possible that she might be pregnant?

Rachel closed her eyes as a wave of panic hit her.
Of course it was possible! She hadn't taken the Pill
since she'd split up with Tom all those years ago;
there'd been no need to worry about birth control
when she hadn't been involved in a relationship.
Shiloh hadn't used any contraception that night, either. They'd been swept away by the intensity of
their feelings and neither of them had given any
thought to the repercussions. Now what was she going to do? How was she going to manage if she was
pregnant? She'd always imagined that when she had
a child it would be within the boundaries of a secure
and loving relationship but that certainly wouldn't
happen now.

She opened her eyes because there was no way
she could hide from the truth. Shiloh didn't want her
so this baby—if, indeed, there was a baby—was her
problem and she couldn't ask him for help.

The weeks passed in a blur. Shiloh lost track of the
time as he immersed himself in a ceaseless round of
work and fundraising. His job as head of surgery at
one of London's most prestigious teaching hospitals
had always been a demanding one and on top of that
he added a non-stop round of dinners and speaking

engagements. Securing funding for Worlds Together had always been very important to him but now he threw himself into the task, body and soul. So long as he kept busy, he reasoned, then he wouldn't have time to think about Rachel.

It was how he'd coped after Sally had died but it was proving far more difficult this time. Whenever he relaxed his guard for a moment thoughts of Rachel came flooding back. He longed to see her but knew how dangerous it would be. If he saw her again, how would he ever find the strength to let her go? The old fears were still there, just as strong as ever, but now there was also the deep sense of loss he felt each day on waking, the feeling that part of him was missing to contend with, and it was exhausting, trying to deal with his own emotions on top of everything else.

He was at a fundraising dinner in Lancaster one evening at the end of October when matters finally came to a head. It was his fifth speaking engagement in less than two weeks. He'd driven straight there after leaving Theatre at lunchtime and was due to drive back to London the same night so he could speak at a lunch the following day. As he stood there, listening to the applause, Shiloh found himself wondering what he was doing. He'd secured sufficient funding now to keep Worlds Together running for several years to come. He could carry on raising money, of course, but eventually his work would suffer. He'd spent the last few months running around in circles and it hadn't got him anywhere so maybe it was time he confronted the problem. He loved Rachel and the last few months had proved that his life wasn't worth a damn if he couldn't share it with her. He had no idea if she and Tom were back together for good but it would be simple enough to find out.

He cut short the evening, thanking his hosts for their generosity and assuring them that he would be in touch. The dinner had been held at a hotel close to the motorway so he got into his car and followed the signs until he came to the junction then headed north towards Dalverston. He had no idea how Rachel would react when he turned up but he wasn't going to let that deter him. He was going to see her, and he swore that if there was a *chance* of getting her back then he wasn't going to let it slip through his fingers. This time he was going to take his courage in both hands and tell her how he felt!

It was gone eight by the time Rachel got home that night. She'd had an appointment with her GP after work, just a routine check-up to monitor her blood pressure and general health. So far she'd been amazingly lucky. The dizzy spells had soon stopped and she'd had none of the usual problems she'd expected, like morning sickness. At five months pregnant she was brimming with health and couldn't remember feeling so well for ages. This baby might not have been planned, she thought, fondly patting her bump, but he was behaving like the perfect textbook child for his mum!

She plugged in the kettle then went to get changed, opting for a pair of soft, grey velvet trousers and a matching top that her friend, Lisa Saunders, had given her. Lisa had arrived one evening with a stack of maternity clothes and had insisted that Rachel must have them. Lisa and Will's son, James, was just six months old and as Lisa had dryly pointed out they weren't planning on having any more babies until James realised that it was possible to sleep through the night without any attention from his mummy and daddy!

It was typical of everyone's attitude because all her friends had been marvellous since they'd found out she was pregnant, offering practical as well as emotional support. She'd told everyone the same story, that she was delighted about the baby even though her relationship with its father hadn't worked out, and nobody had questioned her further. Her niece, Bethany, had offered to come back from Australia as soon as she'd heard the news but Rachel had refused to let her cut short her trip. As she'd told Bethany quite truthfully, she had a lot of support and would manage.

The kettle had boiled by the time she went back to the kitchen so Rachel made herself a cup of tea and drank it before making her supper. She scrambled a couple of eggs and buttered some toast then put everything on a tray and took it through to the sitting room. Even though she felt so well, she tended to tire easily and was looking forward to putting her feet up in front of the television.

She'd just finished her meal when she heard someone ringing the doorbell. It wasn't often that she had visitors of an evening and she frowned as she put the tray on the floor. Lisa had mentioned that she might call round but she usually phoned first so Rachel had no idea who it could be. The very last person she expected to see was Shiloh, and she gasped when she opened the door and found him standing on the step. Shock robbed her of the ability to speak so it was left to him to break the silence.

'Hello, Rachel. I'm sorry to turn up unannounced like this but I needed to speak to you. Can I come in?'

CHAPTER TEN

'I'M BUSY at the moment,' was the first thing she could think of to say.

'Then I promise not to take up too much of your time.'

Shiloh held his smile although it was clear that Rachel wasn't exactly thrilled to see him. Just for a moment he found himself wondering if he'd been mad to come, but there was no way that he was going to give up now he'd got this far. 'Surely you can spare five minutes for a friend?' he said persuasively.

'Friends? Is that what we are?'

She laughed and he winced when he heard the bitter note in her voice. It cut him to the quick to know that he was responsible for it. If he achieved nothing else from this visit then at least he could try and make amends for the way he'd hurt her.

'It's what I hope we can be. I know how hard it must have been for you to understand why I behaved the way I did, but I hope you can find it in your heart to forgive me.'

'There's nothing to forgive,' she said shortly. She started to close the door and Shiloh frowned because it was obvious how reluctant she was to talk to him.

Admittedly, they hadn't parted on the best of terms but it wasn't like Rachel to be so intransigent.

'Well, I think there is, and I've no intention of leaving until I've had the chance to clear up any misunderstandings.' He placed his hand flat on the door and looked her straight in the eyes so there could be no mistake about what he was saying. 'It's your choice, Rachel. We can either talk out here on the doorstep where the world and his wife can listen to what we're saying or you can let me in.'

'Then I suppose you'd better come in, hadn't you?'

She swung round and marched along the hall, leaving him to close the door. Shiloh followed her into the sitting room and looked around. There was nothing at all remarkable about the room but it exuded such a feeling of peace that he immediately felt at home. It was only when he heard the sharpness in her voice that he realised how stupid it was to imagine he was welcome.

'So now that you've blackmailed me into letting you into my home, I'd be grateful if you would tell me what you want so we can get this over with. I've had a really busy day, Shiloh, and I could do without spending my evening playing power games with you!'

'I didn't come here to play games,' he retorted just as sharply because the accusation had stung. He frowned when Rachel didn't even glance at him as she walked to the window and stood there with her back towards him. Did she dislike him so much that she couldn't even bear to look at him? he wondered sadly. It was an effort to continue because the thought had pierced straight through his heart.

'I wanted to see how you were and clear up a few things. That's the only reason I came, Rachel. I certainly didn't come here to upset you.'

'I am not upset!' She half turned then seemed to change her mind and turned back to the window again.

Shiloh studied the rigid set of her back, feeling at a loss to know how to continue. It was obvious how nervous she was about him being there and he couldn't understand what was wrong...

Unless she was worried what Tom would say when he found out he'd been to visit her?

A wave of despair hit him as he realised how stupid he'd been to come. All he'd done was make life even more difficult for Rachel and that was the last thing he'd wanted to do. It was impossible to keep the anguish out of his voice as he apologised.

'I'm sorry. Obviously, it was a mistake to come here tonight. I never meant to upset you, Rachel. I just wanted to...well, clear the air, I suppose, but I can tell that I'm causing more harm than good by being here.'

'What do you mean, that you wanted to clear the

air?' she replied flatly. 'We sorted everything out before we left Mexico so what else is there to say?'

Millions of things, he thought desperately. *I want
to tell you that I love you, that my life is worthless
without you to share it; that when I look into the
future then I can see only darkness because you
won't ever be a part of it.*

The thoughts inside his head were so loud that for
a moment Shiloh thought he'd said them out loud
only Rachel was still standing there, waiting for him
to answer. It took every scrap of strength he possessed not to tell her the truth but he wouldn't risk
causing her any more distress.

'We did but I just I wanted to be sure you were
happy.'

'Happy?' She laughed harshly. 'You came all this
way just to see if I'm *happy*? Oh, please, you can do
better than that!'

'All right, then, I came to see if you and Tom were
back together for good.'

'And what if we are? What business is it of yours?
You made it abundantly clear that you weren't interested in what I did so what makes you think you
have the right to ask about my private life all of a
sudden?'

'I don't have any rights at all. That's perfectly
true.' He summoned a smile although it was difficult
not to let her see how much that accusation had hurt
him. It hadn't been a lack of interest that had made

him push her away—just the opposite, in fact. 'I was in the area and just thought I'd call round to see if things had worked out for you and Tom. That's all there was to it.'

'How very kind of you. Well, I'm sure you'll be delighted to know that everything has worked out just perfectly.'

She turned to face him and Shiloh felt the blood drain from his head when he realised she was pregnant. There was a rushing sound in his ears and his head was pounding as he tried to deal with what he was seeing. It shouldn't have been that difficult, really. Rachel was having Hartley's child and if that wasn't proof of her feelings for the other man then, by heaven, he didn't know what was!

'So I can see. Congratulations.'

'Thank you.' She inclined her head but there was a sparkle of tears in her eyes that surprised him.

'You are pleased about the baby?' he said slowly.

'Of course I am!'

She laid her hand protectively on her belly and Shiloh had to grit his teeth to hold back his cry of anguish. How he wished it was *his* child lying there under her hand, *his* child that she would love and cherish instead of some other man's.

It was all he could do not to tell her the truth—that he loved her and wanted that baby to be his—but what would it achieve? It wouldn't be fair to upset Rachel when she was happy, certainly wouldn't be right to burden her with his grief when she had her future to look forward to. It was the hardest thing he was ever going to have to do but he had to find the strength to be happy for her, too.

'Of course you are,' he agreed, crossing the room. He put his hands on her shoulders, felt the spasm of need that ran through him like lightning and blanked it out as he bent and kissed her gently on the cheek. 'I'm really happy for you, Rachel. Tom is a very lucky man and you can tell him that from me.'

He let her go and headed for the door before he did something he would regret. Rachel had her life back together and he wouldn't spoil it for her. She saw him out then stood on the step to watch as he drove away and he knew that image would be filed away with all the others he had of her. Tears suddenly filled his eyes and he had to stop the car because he couldn't see the road clearly enough to drive. There was a lump in his throat and a hole in his heart because nothing—*nothing!*—had ever hurt as much as this was hurting now.

Rachel was having another man's child and he wanted to rant and rail at fate for making it happen only there was no point. It wouldn't change anything. It certainly wouldn't bring Rachel back or make that child that was growing inside her belong to him.

Rachel sat down on the stairs after Shiloh had left. She felt so sick with guilt that she couldn't stop shaking. The baby must have sensed her turmoil because he started kicking away, showing his displeasure at having his secure little world breached by all these terrible emotions.

She made herself breathe slowly and deeply like the midwife at the antenatal classes she'd been attending had taught her to do and after a while the frantic flutterings inside her began to calm down even if she didn't feel any better. How could she? She hadn't actually *lied* to Shiloh but she'd let him draw his own conclusions about the baby. It had been a lie by omission and she would have to live with the consequences for the rest of her life.

She got up and went into the kitchen to make herself another cup of tea. The kettle boiled and switched itself off but she never even noticed. She couldn't stop thinking about what had just happened. Had she been right to let Shiloh leave, believing that Tom was the baby's father? But what else could she have done? How could she have told him the truth when it would have been the last thing he'd wanted to hear? The deed was done and there could be no going back, although what she would tell the child when he or she was old enough to ask questions was another matter. It was one thing not to tell Shiloh the truth but how could she deliberately lie to her own child about something so important?

Rachel bit her lip as another wave of panic surfaced. It wouldn't be good for the baby if she kept getting upset. She had to stay calm and stick to her decision no matter how difficult it proved to be. After all, Shiloh hadn't come here to tell her that he loved her and wanted her back. He'd come to find out if she'd forgiven him for what had happened in Mexico. He'd been surprised when he'd discovered she was pregnant but by now he was probably feeling relieved that she was no longer his problem. He could safely put what had happened behind him and get on with his life.

Getting on with life proved to be an almost impossible task in the following weeks, Shiloh discovered. He worked harder than ever in an effort to ward off the pain. He virtually doubled the number of hours he spent in Theatre each week and increased his speaking engagements until every night was booked solid. But no matter how hard he worked or how much effort he put into raising funds for the agency, the pain still kept gnawing away at him.

He couldn't stop thinking about Rachel and the baby. He'd always wanted a family of his own although any plans he'd made in the past had been put on ice after Sally's death. Now the need became so strong that he dreamt about the children he would never have—a sturdy little boy with his mop of hair, a pretty little girl with Rachel's beautiful eyes. These dream children were so real that some days he woke up and expected to see them standing by the bed, asking him to play with them. It was pure, unmitigated torture so it was almost a relief when heavy flooding in a remote region of Albania caused dangerous mud slides, burying whole communities. A national disaster was declared and all the usual aid agencies, including Worlds Together, were asked to send teams to the area. Maybe it would help if he put some distance between him and Rachel, gave himself a breathing space while he focused on other people's problems instead of his own.

He set the ball rolling, faxing everyone and booking seats on the plane then arranging for their equipment to be flown out. He never knew who would be able to make it on any mission but the response was excellent and he ended up turning people down.

They flew out of Heathrow at seven a.m. one drizzly November morning and by lunchtime that same day were hard at work. There were hundreds of people injured and the continuing floods meant that the local infrastructure had fallen into disarray. Hospitals throughout the region had been cut off by flood water and were suffering from power shortages. Shiloh and his team picked up as much of the work as they could but it was hard going and they were soon exhausted. However, when a message arrived from a village right up in the mountains that a doctor was desperately needed, he didn't hesitate.

He took one of their trucks and set off for the village. Mike Rafferty had volunteered to go with him and he was glad of the company because the roads were dreadful. They were almost there when Shiloh heard a rumbling sound from above and looked up to see a vast curtain of mud bearing down on them. There was no time to do anything before it swept them down the mountainside and his last thought before he passed out was that he wished he'd told Rachel that he loved her.

Rachel was in the canteen having her lunch when Caroline came to find her. She groaned when the trainee came hurrying over to her table. 'Don't tell me someone else has gone off sick?'

'No, it's nothing like that,' Caroline explained quickly. 'There's someone on the phone for you. She says it's really urgent and that she needs to speak to you right away.'

'I don't suppose you managed to get her name, did you?' Rachel asked wearily, getting up.

'Yes, of course I did. Natalie Palmer.'

'Natalie? Good heavens, I wonder what she wants?'

Rachel quickly left the canteen. She hadn't spoken to Natalie since they'd been in Mexico together and couldn't imagine why she needed to speak to her so urgently. She went down in the lift with Caroline and hurried to her office.

'Natalie? It's Rachel.'

'Oh, thank heavens you're there. Look, Rachel,

there's no easy way to tell you this but Shiloh has been hurt. He's in a really bad way.'

'Hurt? But how? What's happened?' Rachel demanded. She sat down abruptly as her legs suddenly gave way.

'He and Rafferty were caught up in a mud slide. They were in Albania, helping out after the recent flooding. They were on their way to one of the villages when their truck was swept down the side of a mountain.'

'Oh, no! How bad are they?' Rachel bit her lip when she felt tears fill her eyes. The thought of Shiloh having been injured was more than she could bear.

'Rafferty isn't too bad, apparently,' Natalie explained with a catch in her voice. 'It's Shiloh who's fared the worst, I'm afraid. He was driving when it happened and he suffered severe crush injuries from the steering-wheel.'

Rachel gulped. 'So what's happening? Are they being treated over there or are they being brought back home?'

'They're being flown back today. Conditions over there are still pretty grim, apparently, and David Preston wants to get Shiloh back home as soon as possible.'

'I see. What time are they due to arrive?'

'This afternoon, which is why I'm phoning you. Is there any chance that you would come to London?

Evidently, Shiloh regained consciousness for a short time and started asking for you. He's now lapsed back into a coma but David feels that it might help if you went to see him. I know it's a lot to ask, Rachel…'

'Of course I'll come! Just tell me which hospital and I'll be there.'

'Thanks, Rachel. I can't tell you what a relief it is. I've been out of my mind with worry, what with Rafferty being injured as well…' Natalie broke off and swallowed. 'Anyway, they're being taken to St Leonard's, where Shiloh works. D'you know where it is?'

'No, but I'll find it. Don't worry.'

Rachel was trembling when she hung up. She couldn't bear to imagine Shiloh lying in a hospital bed when he'd always been so strong, so vital, so…so *alive*. She took a deep breath then picked up the phone again. This wasn't the time to panic because she needed to arrange cover before she could leave. It caused a bit of a rumpus when she asked for time off but she was adamant that she was going so in the end the nursing officer agreed to bring in an agency nurse. Her relief arrived twenty minutes later so Rachel handed over the ward to her and left. She'd already phoned the station by then and knew there was a train to London leaving within the hour so she took a taxi straight there.

The train was on time for once so three hours later

she was in another taxi, heading for the hospital. Natalie met her in Reception and they hugged each other, tears streaming down their faces as they clung together for a few moments.

Natalie blew her nose and smiled. 'We're a right pair. Look at the state of us.' She wiped her eyes then gasped when she looked at Rachel. 'You're pregnant!'

'Yes, I know.' Rachel laughed. 'Sorry. I just never thought to mention it.'

'I wish you had. I feel awful now about asking you to come all this way. Are you sure you're all right?'

'I'm fine, or I will be once I've seen Shiloh,' she said firmly.

'They arrived about an hour ago. I haven't seen either of them yet because the doctors are with them. All I know is that Rafferty has umpteen fractures and that Shiloh is still unconscious.'

'How soon can I see him?' Rachel demanded anxiously.

'I don't know. He's been taken to ICU so they'll probably want to do some tests after they get him settled in.' Natalie managed a watery smile. 'We both know the routine, don't we?'

'Yes, although I'm not sure if that makes it easier or worse. Ignorance can be bliss sometimes.'

'I know what you mean.' Natalie pointed to the coffee-shop at the far side of the foyer. 'Let's sit down and have a drink while we wait. I managed to beg a pager off one of the nurses and she's promised to call me when there's any news.'

Rachel could see the sense in that so she went and sat down while Natalie fetched their drinks. She was impatient to see Shiloh but it wouldn't help the staff to do their job if she started pestering them. Natalie came back with two caffe-lattes and put them on the table.

'So when is the baby due?' she asked, sitting down.

'The end of February,' Rachel replied, stirring sugar into her coffee.

'Really? So that means you were pregnant when you went to Mexico?'

'No.' Rachel put the spoon on the saucer and took a deep breath. She couldn't have explained it but she knew that this wasn't the time to lie. 'I got pregnant while I was in Mexico and, contrary to any rumours you may have heard, it had nothing whatsoever to do with Tom Hartley.'

'Are you saying what I think you are?' Natalie demanded incredulously.

'Yes.' Rachel sighed. 'It's Shiloh's baby although he doesn't know that.'

'And when were you planning on telling him?' Natalie gasped when Rachel blushed. 'You weren't going to tell him, were you, Rachel? You were going to let him think it was this other man's child.'

'I know it sounds awful but it seemed the best thing to do. Shiloh made it clear that he wasn't interested and there was no room in his life for me…'

'Rubbish! Oh, I'm not claiming he didn't say that because I know how stubborn he can be when he gets an idea into his head. Show me a man who isn't! But he's crazy about you, Rachel, so please, *please*, I beg you not to take any notice if he tells you he doesn't need you. He's just scared stiff of losing you the way he lost Sally.'

'But he virtually pushed me and Tom together!'

'Because he probably thought he was doing the right thing.' Natalie sighed. 'It's so typical of Shiloh to do something like that.'

Rachel could barely believe what she was hearing. Was it possible that Natalie was right? It was hard to believe and yet, thinking about that visit he'd paid her, it seemed to add up. By the time a message arrived to say they could see the men, Rachel's head was spinning from trying to make sense of it all. She and Natalie went up in the lift together although Natalie got out on the fifth floor while she carried on to the IC unit. The sister on duty took her through, briefly explaining that she mustn't worry about all the machinery. Rachel didn't bother explaining that she was a nurse because it didn't matter. The only thing that mattered was the man lying in the bed.

She sat down on a chair beside the bed and covered Shiloh's hand with hers. His skin was cool but she could feel his pulse tapping away beneath her fingertips and that was reassuring. Her eyes skimmed over him, taking note of the signs of recent major surgery, the pallor of his skin, and a lump came to her throat. She loved him so much and she would never forgive herself if anything happened and she hadn't told him that this child she was carrying was his.

Bending, she placed her lips against his ear, willing him to hear what she was saying. Nobody really knew if a patient in a coma could hear or not, although there'd been many reports of people waking and reporting what had been said to them. But if there was any chance that Shiloh might be able to hear her then it was worth doing.

'Shiloh, this baby is yours,' she whispered. 'It's *your* child, *your* son or *your* daughter. I hope you can hear me because I know that you'll fight all the harder to get better then. The baby and I need you here with us, my darling. We love you.'

Her voice broke and she buried her face in his arm. It had to work because she couldn't bear to lose him.

CHAPTER ELEVEN

RACHEL stayed in the IC unit all night long. Shiloh was still unconscious and the constant beeping of the monitor was an ever-present reminder that his life was hanging in the balance. When the day staff arrived, she reluctantly agreed to leave while they made him comfortable. Of course, she could have done a lot of the tasks herself—cleaned his eyes and wiped his lips with a moistened cotton ball, checked his drip—but the nursing side of her seemed to have been suspended. She was just another anxious relative waiting for her loved one to wake up and the tension was unbearable.

She went to the relatives' room, fed coins into the machine and waited while it chugged out a cup of insipid-looking tea. She knew she really should eat something for the baby's sake but she just wasn't hungry. She drank her tea then sat and stared at the wall until one of the nurses came to fetch her. Shiloh looked a little better when she went back, not quite so pale and his breathing seemed steadier as well. Rachel kissed him on the forehead and told him how much she loved him and needed him to get better. Maybe he could hear her and maybe he couldn't but it made *her* feel better to imagine that something of what she was saying might be getting through.

Natalie popped in during the morning to tell her that Rafferty was fine. He had a fractured femur, a hairline fracture to his clavicle and badly bruised ribs but he'd survive. Rachel made all the right responses but she was glad when Natalie left because she wanted to be on her own with Shiloh.

She held his hand and told him about the baby and what they would do when he was well enough to leave hospital. Maybe they were pipe dreams but they were her dreams and she wanted to share them with him. She must have dozed off eventually, worn out by the sleepless night and worry, and in her dreams she and Shiloh were playing with their son in the garden, laughing as they chased him across the grass...

It was such a wonderful dream. He could hear a child laughing and could see Rachel's smiling face as she turned to look at him. She was trying to tell him something but although he could see her mouth moving he couldn't hear the words. He struggled to hear what she was saying but something was getting in the way...

Shiloh woke with a start, his heart thumping the way it did after a dream. His head felt fuzzy and there was a gnawing pain in the centre of his chest that got worse when he tried to sit up. He groaned as he sank back against the pillows, wondering what was wrong with him…and that was when he realised he wasn't in his own bed. His eyes swivelled first left then right in panic. Bare cream walls one way and a load of machinery the other. What the hell was going on?

'Shiloh? Are you awake? Can you hear me, darling? Don't try to speak. Just nod your head or squeeze my fingers or…or something!'

'Rachel?' His voice sounded horrible, all rough and gravelly, although it wasn't surprising when his throat was so swollen. Rachel must have heard him, however, because all of a sudden her face came into view.

'I'm right here, sweetheart. We both are. Me and the baby.'

She was smiling at him just like in his dream but there were tears running down her face as well. Shiloh frowned because he couldn't bear to see her looking so unhappy.

'Don't cry. Please, don't cry,' he muttered gruffly.

'I'm crying because I'm happy not because I'm sad.' She kissed him gently on the forehead and he closed his eyes because it was so wonderful that it felt as though he'd died and gone to heaven…

His eyes flew open and he stared at her in alarm. 'I'm dead, aren't I? That's why I imagined you just kissed me.'

'Of course you aren't dead!' She chuckled as she

gently—ever so gently—brushed her mouth against his. 'You're in hospital, darling. You had an accident while you were driving and had to be flown back home to London.'

'I remember now,' he said slowly, piecing it all together. 'Mike and I were driving along this mountain road when a great wall of mud came rushing down…' He stopped and swallowed. 'What's happened to Mike?'

'Mike is fine. He's in the surgical ward, two floors below. Natalie's with him.'

'Thank heavens!' He heaved a sigh of relief then groaned when pain stabbed through his chest.

'Poor you. You must feel awful. I'll get one of the staff to sort out some extra pain relief.' Rachel tenderly stroked his cheek. 'You suffered crush injuries from bouncing off the steering-wheel but David managed to put everything back together, I believe.'

'That's good,' he mumbled. His head was starting to feel dreadfully fuzzy again. He tried to stave off the blackness but it was creeping up on him once more. Rachel brushed another feather-light kiss over his forehead and he wanted to protest that he needed a real kiss only he didn't have the strength. It would have to wait till later, he decided as he slipped back into unconsciousness. Later when he felt better and could kiss her back…

It was evening when Shiloh next awoke and he felt far more alert. He looked right then left, checking

that he hadn't dreamt the machinery and dismal
paintwork, but everything was much as it had been
the first time around. A smile tilted his mouth as he
waited for Rachel to appear but several seconds
passed and there was no sign of her. Sadness settled
over him like a dark cloud as he realised that he must
have dreamt her. His mind had conjured her up because he'd wanted so desperately to see her.

'Ah, so you're back with us again. Good.'

Shiloh turned his head and frowned when he saw
the nurse who was changing his drip. 'How long was
I unconscious?'

'Oh, a good forty-eight hours from what I can
gather, Dr Smith.' She hooked a fresh bag onto the
stand then altered the settings on the machine.
'That's better. Miss Hart has just popped out for a
few minutes but she shouldn't be long, and Mr Lewis
will be here very shortly to check you over.'

She turned to leave but Shiloh had to stop her.
'Wait! What d'you mean, Miss Hart has just popped
out? She was really here and I didn't imagine her?'

'You most certainly didn't!' The nurse laughed
kindly. 'She's been here all day and most of yesterday as well. I had the devil of a job persuading her
to take a break, in fact.'

Shiloh closed his eyes after the nurse left. He
couldn't believe what he'd heard. Rachel had been
here all that time? If it was true then it meant that
he hadn't dreamt her and that she really *had* kissed

him and called him sweetheart. His mind struggled back through the mist and he started to remember other things as well, things that made his heart race. Were they also true? Was it possible that this baby she was having was really his?

It was too much to take in. When he saw Rachel approaching, he was overwhelmed by the magnitude of it all. It was as though he was about to have his dearest wish granted and he was afraid—so very afraid—that it might not happen, and he couldn't bear it. Tears filled his eyes and he heard Rachel's murmur of concern as she bent over him.

'Darling, what is it? Are you in pain? Let me get the doctor—'

'No!' He grasped her hand and clung onto it, praying that he wasn't about to face the worst moment of his life when he felt the least able to deal with it. 'I don't need the doctor. I just need you to tell me if it's true.'

'Is what true?' she began, then stopped.

Shiloh saw the colour flow up her face and his heart ran wild, causing the monitor to beep like crazy. He could hear the sound of footsteps as the staff came hurrying over but he didn't even glance their way. His eyes were locked to Rachel's face, held there by the intensity of his need.

'Is the baby mine, Rachel?' he asked softly, so softly, in fact, that he wondered for a horrible moment if she could hear him, but he needn't have worried. She took his hand and placed it on the swollen mound of her belly.

'Yes. This is your son or your daughter, Shiloh. *Our* child.'

There wasn't time to say anything else because the staff had arrived, politely but firmly asking Rachel to leave while they checked him over. She stepped away from the bed and smiled as she mouthed the words 'I love you' over everyone's head.

Shiloh closed his eyes, ignoring the indignities that were being performed upon his person by the nursing staff. They were just concerned about him but they needn't have worried because he was going to make the most miraculous recovery known to man. He had the best incentive in the world to get better. Rachel and his child, and a whole new life the three of them were going to build together.

Rachel hired a car to take Shiloh home once he was well enough to leave the hospital. The consultant in charge of the IC unit had told her that he'd never seen a patient recover so quickly before. Rachel had forborne to tell him that few people had the kind of incentive that Shiloh had and just thanked heaven that he was well enough to go home, but she knew that she would never doubt the power of love again.

They drove back to his flat and used the lift rather than climbing the stairs because Shiloh still needed to be careful. His chest was healing well but they'd been warned that he would need several months to recover fully from his injuries. Rachel had taken leave of absence from work and had been staying in the flat so she let them in then chivvied him into the sitting room.

'Sit down and put your feet up,' she instructed, moving the footstool in front of the sofa. 'I'll make us some coffee or maybe you'd prefer tea…'

'What I'd *prefer* is a kiss.' His smile was wicked and wonderfully sexy as he pulled her down beside him and she frowned in concern.

'Now, remember what the consultant told you—'

'To hell with that. Lewis is an old fusspot,' he growled, pulling her towards him. He kissed her tenderly on the mouth then sighed. 'Oh, that's better! I am sick and tired of trying to snatch the odd moment on our own. I never realised before how difficult it is to have any privacy when you're in hospital.'

'You were there to get better,' she reminded him primly, and he snorted.

'I'd have got better a lot faster if I'd been able to do this.'

This was another kiss, far more passionate this time so that Rachel sighed dreamily when it ended. 'Mmm, you may have a point.'

'I *know* I have a point.' His hand skimmed down her throat and she saw him smile when he discovered how fast her pulse was beating. It obviously encouraged him to explore further and she shuddered when she felt his fingers brushing her nipples.

'You need to rest,' she reminded him again, although it wasn't easy to be the sensible one all the time. 'Mr Lewis said it was most important that you didn't tire yourself out.'

'I don't intend to.' He kissed her softly then found the hem of her T-shirt and let his hands sneak beneath it. 'I give you my word that I won't dig the garden or run for a bus. I won't even go into work until Mr Lewis says I can.'

'Really?' She looked at him in surprise.

'Really.' He kissed her again, gently nibbling her lower lip until she opened her mouth for him. They had to stop talking for a moment and it was hard to remember what they'd been saying once the kiss had ended.

'I don't have a garden, never use the bus and I have far too many other things to do instead of going to work.'

'Oh, I see,' she murmured. 'What sort of "other things" did you have in mind, though? I mean, I might just have to veto them if they are too strenuous.'

'I'm not planning on doing anything too strenuous—at the moment.'

Rachel gasped when she realised he'd managed to unfasten the clasp on her bra while they'd been talking. He cupped her breasts in his hands and she shuddered when she felt his thumbs rubbing her nipples. Her breasts were incredibly sensitive now and the sensation was almost too intense to bear. When he dragged the T-shirt over her head then pulled her to him so he could suckle her, she cried out as a wave of desire swept through her.

Rachel buried her fingers in his hair and held his head against her as their desire grew. Every sweep of his tongue made her body throb as though it was in torment but it was the sweetest agony imaginable. She pressed herself against him, feeling the hardness of his arousal then gasped when the baby suddenly kicked her hard in the ribs.

Shiloh froze and she saw his face fill with wonderment. 'It's amazing. I could actually feel him kicking!'

'I don't know why you're so surprised,' she said tenderly. 'You *are* a doctor so I assume you've read all the textbooks.'

'I have but it's different when it's your own child, isn't it?'

His voice was husky with joy and her eyes prickled with sudden tears when she realised how awful it would have been if he'd never found out the truth. She was filled with shame about what she had done and he must have sensed something was wrong. He tilted her face up and made her look at him.

'What is it? Tell me what you're thinking, Rachel.

I don't want there to be any secrets between us ever again.'

'I'm so sorry that I let you think this was Tom's baby. I'll never forgive myself. I just didn't know what to say for the best at the time…'

'Hush!' He drew her into his arms and gently rocked her. 'We both made mistakes although I made a lot more than you so there's no need to feel guilty. You did what you thought was best for everyone and I'm only glad that I found out the truth in the end.'

'I didn't want to lie to you. I just thought it would be wrong to tell you because if you didn't want me then you wouldn't want our child either. But I swear that nothing went on between me and Tom apart from that one kiss you witnessed.'

'I'm glad although it wouldn't have changed how I feel even if something had happened.'

'What do you mean?'

'That I love you, Rachel, and what went on in the past is all part and parcel of who you are today. But it won't ever change how I feel about you.'

'Thank you.' She kissed him on the mouth, held him close for a second then sat back because it was important they got this clear from the beginning. 'I feel the same about you, darling. I know how much you loved Sally and I swear that I won't ever try to take her place.'

'I have some wonderful memories of Sally and the time we had together. I'll always keep a special place in my heart for her but it's time I moved on.' He framed her face between his hands and his gaze was fierce all of a sudden. 'I love you now, Rachel. I want to go to sleep each night with you in my arms and wake up each morning still holding you. You and our baby are the two most precious, most wonderful things that have ever happened to me.'

'Oh, Shiloh, I don't know what to say. I never imagined I could be this happy.'

'Neither did I which makes it all the more important that we don't ever lose sight of how lucky we are. We came so close to losing one another and there is no way I want to risk that happening again.'

He kissed her tenderly then set her away from him and she shivered when she saw the burning light in his eyes. 'I want to spend my life with you, Rachel, so will you marry me?'

'I… Oh…yes! Yes!'

'Then come here and let's seal this in the time-honoured fashion,' he growled, pulling her towards him.

'But, Shiloh, your chest…'

'My chest will be fine. It's a completely different part of my anatomy that you need to worry about!'

One month later…

'You look beautiful, Rachel. Really, beautiful.'

'Do you think so?'

Rachel stepped in front of the mirror and studied herself critically, taking stock of the simple, floor-length, cream silk gown. Shiloh had insisted that they shouldn't wait until after the baby was born before they got married so they had pulled out all the stops and got the wedding arranged as quickly as possible. The only drawback so far as Rachel was concerned was that there was no hiding the fact that she was pregnant. However, she didn't look *too* bad, considering.

She turned her head to the side and smiled when she saw the tiny white flowers that Lisa had woven into her hair. She'd decided not to carry a bouquet but her friend had insisted that she should have flowers and had come up with the idea of wearing them in her hair. Bethany, had lent her a dainty, silver heart necklace as the something borrowed part of the old wedding tradition and Natalie had provided the something blue in the form of a pair of saucy lace panties which Rachel was wearing under her gown. Natalie had brushed aside her protests that a woman who was eight months pregnant couldn't possibly look sexy with the assurance that Shiloh wouldn't agree. Now Rachel shivered because that was very true. As he'd shown her very graphically only last night that he didn't find her pregnancy the least bit offputting.

'OK. I think I'm ready. Shall we go?'

She turned away from the mirror, suddenly impatient to get the ceremony under way. The sooner she got to the church, the sooner she and Shiloh could be married and that was what she wanted more than anything. They were holding the service in the chapel at Dalverston General and there were a lot of familiar faces lining the corridor when Rachel arrived. Every member of staff who could possibly find an excuse to slip away had made their way there, it seemed.

Will Saunders, Lisa's husband, had offered to give her away and he was waiting by the chapel door. He grinned at her. 'There's still time to change your mind.'

'No way!' she declared as the doors opened. The place was packed and she spotted June, Brian and Alison among the crowd crammed into the pews. So many people had wanted to wish her and Shiloh well for the future and she was deeply touched.

The organist struck up the opening chords of the wedding march and they started walking down the aisle. Shiloh stepped out of the front pew and turned to watch her and the expression on his face made her heart overflow with happiness. She quickened her pace, wanting to get to him as quickly as she could so they could start on the next phase of their life together and he met her halfway, taking her hands and kissing them, then kissing her on the mouth so there was hardly a dry eye in the place by the time the priest began the service. Their love for one another was so great that it touched everyone present.

Rachel clung to his hand as she repeated her vows before all their friends. She meant every word, knew that Shiloh meant them as well. 'To have and to hold...from this day forward...forsaking all others...' They were the promises so many people had made over the years but they were new and special to them. When the priest finally declared them man and wife Shiloh swept her into his arms as a cheer erupted.

Rachel could feel the baby kicking inside her as she kissed him and knew that she was the luckiest woman in the world. She had the man she loved with her whole heart and soon she would have his child.

'I love you,' she whispered, smiling into his eyes.

'And I love you, too,' he replied, then kissed her again.

Watch out for exciting new covers on your favourite books!

Every month we bring you romantic
fiction that you love!
Now it will be even easier to find your favourite
book with our **fabulous new covers!**

We've listened to you – our loyal readers, and as of
July publications you'll find that...

We've improved:

- ☑ *Variety between the books*
- ☑ *Ease of selection*
- ☑ *Flashes or symbols to highlight mini-series and themes*

We've kept:

- ☑ *The familiar cover colours*
- ☑ *The series names you know*
- ☑ *The style and quality of the stories you love*

Be sure to look out for next months titles so that you can preview our exciting new look.

MILLS & BOON®

0704/RE-LAUNCH/MB

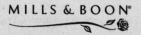

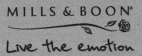

MILLS & BOON®

Live the emotion

Medical Romance™

THE DOCTOR'S UNEXPECTED FAMILY
by Lilian Darcy

The last thing Caroline Archer was looking for was romance – so she was surprised to feel attraction for her new colleague, Declan McCulloch. It was a friendship that quickly developed into a passion – and with that passion Caroline held a secret, a secret that would keep Declan in Glenfallon for ever…

HIS PREGNANT GP *by Lucy Clark*

When Dr Jake Carson takes a position in a small town practice in Australia, he expects his pace of life to slow down. But when Jake discovers that the sexy, single and pregnant Dr Rebekah Sanderson is his new partner and housemate, he suddenly finds himself in at the deep end!

THE ENGLISH DOCTOR'S BABY *by Sarah Morgan*

Alex Westerling is a brilliant doctor. He's also never out of the celebrity magazines – he's an aristocrat with a string of women lining up behind him! That's until beautiful nurse Jenny Phillips turns up on his doorstep, claiming that her late sister's baby is *his* child!

On sale 7th May 2004

Available at most branches of WHSmith, Tesco, Martins, Borders, Eason, Sainsbury's and all good paperback bookshops.

0404/03a

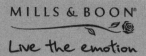